To Jim & Billie B.
I hope you en
is about being
becomes rough. Hang tough and
God bless!

Tom Whatley

MAR 22, 2001

Tom is long time friend and
pastor of woodward ave
Baptist church muscle shoals

Jim

Cuts No Slack

Cuts No Slack

Tom V. Whatley

SUNSTONE
PRESS

SANTA FE

Sunstone books may be purchased for educational, business, or sales promotional use. For information please write: Special Markets Department, Sunstone Press, P.O. Box 2321, Santa Fe, New Mexico 87504-2321.

FIRST EDITION

10 9 8 7 6 5 4 3 2 1

———————————————————————————

    Library of Congress Cataloging-in-Publication Data:
Whatley, Tom V., 1940–
    Cuts no slack / Tom V. Whatley. — 1st ed.
        p. cm.
    ISBN: 0-86534-316-0
    1. Texas—Fiction. 2. Arizona—Fiction. I. Title.

PS3573. H33 C87 2000
813' .54--dc21   00-041935

———————————————————————————

Published by SUNSTONE PRESS
                Post Office Box 2321
                Santa Fe, NM 87504-2321 / USA
                (505) 988-4418 / *orders only* (800) 243-5644
                FAX (505) 988-1025
                www.sunstonepress.com

For Roslyn
with whom I have created a strong family
for thirty eight years
and Jeff R. (Bud) Cummings,
my hero since I was a child.

1850s, somewhere in eastern Arizona

The wind picked at my face and told me the weather was changing. A brief chill ran down my spine. I sat in the shadows of the trees lining a ridge that formed the western boundary of a wide valley. I could hear my horses cropping grass behind me.

Through the eyeglass cradled in my hands, I carefully studied the valley floor. I had come into the valley from a mountain to the east and I focused my attention on that spot. Upon entering the valley I had worked my way across it, stopping only to water my mount and my packhorse in the small stream that meandered through the tall rich grass that blanketed it. I could still make out the trail my horses left in the grass over an hour earlier.

The wind swirled in the tree tops singing a tune that had always been one of my favorites. I thought of hot coffee and a warm fire. I had left last night's camp before light and had not taken time to eat. For two days my neck had been itching and my senses had a shell in the chamber with the hammer back. It was just a feeling, but one that had served me well many times before.

Two deer moved out into the grass and began to graze slowly toward the stream. Deer are always aware of what is around them. I had learned as a boy, while hunting for meat, that if you are ever upwind of them you can forget it. Their sense of hearing is about as good.

These deer were fidgety as they ate. One of them always had its head up in the wind and looking around. Suddenly both deer raised their heads and looked directly at the spot where I had entered the valley. They flashed their tails and bounded off into the trees.

I rose quickly and gathered the reins of my horse. I caught up the lead rope of my pack horse, swung into the saddle, and rode out of there without looking back. As I topped the ridge heading west I smiled to myself and thought, your neck was right again Bud. I wanted to put some distance between me and whoever was back there before nightfall.

The wind blew cold along the Mogollon rim that runs like a knife slash through the eastern side of Arizona. Huddled by a small fire and back against a bluff that was surrounded by tall pines and a lot of deadfall, I pondered my journey toward the red hills I had heard my paw talk about. He had gone through there coming back from California a few years ago. We had set up late into the nights listening to his tales and it set my heart longing to see them for myself.

Paw had really set to wandering after maw died. I was twelve when we laid her to rest under a clump of Texas liveoaks on the hill behind our ranch house along the Brazos river. Maw had been a good woman. She had never complained as she tried to survive living with a man that didn't like being hitched down. Paw always said he liked being married, but he needed a long rope tied to him because he liked to keep moving. Maw, my sister Tess, and me—we spent most of our days looking for paw to come home from his wanderings. Up til the fever got maw they lasted for six months at a time maybe. But his desire to see the big ocean and California, after maw died, took him nearly a year.

Me and Tess kept things going the best we could. We had a couple hundred head of brood cows, a few good bulls, about twenty head of horses, and two old mules. Tess was two years older than me and took to bossing like crazy. During those long days of listening to her telling me to do this and do that, I swore I'd never get tied down to a woman permanent. We done a lot of things together like gathering and moving the cows, branding, and taking them to sell when buyers didn't come by the place. She done most of the woman work and I done most of the fixing up that was always there to face a man come daylight every day.

Well, when paw come home from one of his trips with his talk of California, he caught me at a time when I was fairly fed up with ranching. Fed up with a bossy sister. Fed up with mesquite and rattlesnakes. Fed up with being locked into that Brazos lowland that seemed like a mile high fence. I guess I had my paw's blood in me alright cause when he got to talking them red hills I caught myself daydreaming every day. For weeks I'd set and picture them hills and wonder what it would be like to see them up close. Paw talked about how trees would grow on some of them and how some looked like different colors of red cut in slabs and stacked on top of each other like flapjacks.

When I couldn't stand it any longer, I up and told paw I was leaving to go see them. I figured I'd better tell him before he left out

9

again and I'd be stuck with the job of not being able to leave Tess and the ranch. Paw laughed when I told him and said he figured I'd get tired of nursing them cows one day.

So I packed me a horse with supplies and saddled my horse. I lit out of that Brazos country over a year ago. It wasn't hard to leave, but it has been a mite lonely. I'll admit there's been a few times when I would have loved to hear Tess bossing me around just to hear somebody talk. I guess loneliness is normal to an eighteen year old boy who wants to be a man, yet is all alone.

So, here I sit by a hat-sized fire on a icy cold night, wondering what tomorrow would hold for me. Somebody had been on my trail for about three days. That's why the fire was small and why I was slumped down by the fire in a small depression almost like a bowl. The trees were thick around me and the deadfall plenty to make a feller let me know he was coming if he tried to injun up on me. The wood for my fire was dry and there was little smoke.

You could stand on the bluff above me and not see me or the horses cause the bluff sloped back in as it got close to the ground. Watching my horses for any kind of warning and listening for any sound that would give away a feller trying to sneak up on me, I told myself, I don't guess you'll sleep much tonight.

Rolled up in my blanket against the chill as my fire died down, my mind drifted back to those days along the Brazos. There had been a part of me that few folks had ever seen.

My name is Reed Haddok, but maw and paw had taken to calling me Bud from before I could remember. So, Bud Haddok was who I was. My grandpaw, Reedus Haddok, who had been a blacksmith and metal man back east in Tennessee, was where I got my name. I don't know where my folks got Bud.

My paw used to say as I was growing up, "Bud, I'd better not ever catch you causing trouble to no man, woman, or kid. If I ever do, I'll tan your hide. But if trouble ever comes your way, you don't cut it no slack." My paw was a rough and tumble fighter and the word was that he could pretty well hold his own. He taught me to feint with the left and throw the right. He taught me to throw a hip roll and stomp a man's foot. Over and over he told me, "When you throw a punch, roll your shoulder and punch through what you are trying to hit." He taught me that gettin knocked down was the easiest thing about fighting, but gettin back up was the hardest. He would say, "Just keep gettin up til you see quit in his eyes." We went at it enough up til I was about sixteen and then of a sudden paw stopped teaching me. He said he saw something in my eyes that made him a little nervous. I think it was the day I rolled him pretty hard and he got up slow. I found myself at the edge of hurting him real bad. He was the first to see that part of me.

The second time that part of me rose up was in the fall of my

11

sixteenth year. I was six feet two and weighed about one hundred eighty-five pounds. The years of cuttin wood, throwin cows, building dams, and hard work of the ranch left me what paw called mostly muscle and gristle. Paw had been gone about two weeks on one of his see the world trips and me and Tess was taking care of the chores. I was down by the pole corral fixin a gate when I heard horses coming. I turned and before I could move toward my rifle that was leaning against the barn three men rode right up to where I was standing. Their horses carried the Lazy L brand and I knew they were from the outfit west of the Brazos. Our place lay east of the Brazos and that old river served as a pretty good fence although we had to keep check on our stock and run them back across when they rambled over on Lazy L land. I didn't know these fellers. The one sittin right above me, lookin down on me, was the one who spoke.

"That old brindle bull of yours crossed over onto Lazy L land and got in a fight with Mr. Larkin's best bull. He horned our bull pretty good and he might die from it. We rode over here to tell you that I shot and killed your bull and we are going to shoot any more of your stock that crosses the Brazos."

Now they seemed pretty sure of themselves. I thought I saw one of them smile a bit when they spoke of killing old Brindle. Well, I felt it rising. While that feller was finishing his words, in one swift movement, I reached up with my left hand and jerked him out of the saddle. He fell right on his head and I pulled my knife from my belt and reached and got a handful of his hair. By the time their horses settled down from the commotion and they got their guns out, I had that knife against the throat of their pal and I said calmly, as if I

12

didn't have a care in the world, "This knife is razor sharp and it will cut clean through his neck with one pull."

The feller I was holding was out cold from the fall, but the other two looked like they thought they were still in control of things. I moved that knife ever so gently toward me and a thin line of blood started seeping down his throat. One of them said, "Wait a minute kid. Don't kill him. Give him to us and we'll hightail it out of here."

I had not moved. I looked at them for a few seconds and saw the quit come into their eyes. I then spoke quietly, "If you had told me my bull was over there, I would have driven him back. I can't keep two bulls from fighting. If my bull had caused you damage, I would have stood for it. You two ride out of here and be back by dark with a bull to replace mine or I'm gonna cut his throat." They started to talk again and I just drew that knife a little more across his throat. They whirled and rode out of there like the devil was after them.

I drug the man over by the fence and tied his hands to a post. I fetched a bucket of water and doused him with it. He began to move and moan a little. I wet a rag and washed the blood off his neck. I had not cut him deep, but a scratch there will bleed real good. It looked worse than it was. The thing that kind of bothered me was I knew I would have cut his throat if I had to.

I got back to work and had to listen to that gent cuss me, beg me, and a few times he got so worked up he cried. Tess had seen the whole thing from the house and I learned later she had a rifle on them and swore she could have handled the other two if she needed to. She said to me, "Bud, are you crazy? You must be, takin on three armed men with a knife."

"It seems like they took me on. If I had cut'em some slack, they'd be runnin all over us."

I told her to stay in the house and give me some cover if I needed it. I took my rifle and walked over to the shade of a liveoak and set down to wait. It was gettin late in the afternoon when I heard them comin. I eased to my feet and walked over to where the feller was tied to the fence. By this time he was babbling and looked a mess.

Eight riders crossed the river with two of them half pulling and half being pulled by a big old longhorn bull. The man in front pulled up short and said, "I'm Cyrus Larkin." He said it like it ought to mean something to me. I just stood there with that rifle pointed right at his cowhand, who at the time was begging his boss to cut him loose.

Larkin spoke again, "I don't hold to my men shooting your bull. They didn't do that on my orders. They will work for the price of this bull I'm bringing you and believe me, it will take them a while to pay for it."

I still had not said a word. The hammer on my rifle was eared back and my finger rested tightly on the trigger. Finally, I said, "Put the bull in the corral and cut your man loose." As they started to move, I decided to tell them where we stood. "We take care of our place and our stock. We don't aim to cause trouble for nobody. But if you or anybody else brings trouble to us, you'll get all you want and then some."

Larkin spoke, "I check you folks out every now and then. You got a small spread, but you run it real good. You take care of your stock in the winter and you are producing some good steers."

Just as I was about to relax in all his honey-drippin words he went and stepped over the line again.

"There's no telling what you folks could do if that no-account daddy of yours would stay around and help you."

My trigger finger tightened on that rifle and I swung it swiftly til it was pointed right at his belly. "Mr Larkin, my paw taught me everything I know from cows to fighting. He ain't no-account. If I ever hear you say that about him agin, I'll find you and I'll kill you."

"I'm sorry son. Accept my apology. I had no call to talk about your paw like that." He looked at this sixteen year old kid with amazement for a spell. Then he said, "I'd be kinda proud to know I had a son like you."

I noticed a smile on his face as he motioned his men to put the bull in the corral and to cut their pal loose. They put him on his horse and rode out slowly. I watched them til they crossed the Brazos.

Tess walked down to where I was standing and after a few minutes of silence, we walked over to the corral.

"He's a fine bull," she said.

"Yep! I guess he'll do."

As we turned to walk back to the house I noticed she was looking at me like something was wrong with me.

About a month later paw rode in and wouldn't you know, the first thing he noticed was that new longhorn bull.

"Where'd you git him?"

"I made a trade," I said and walked away. That night after I went to bed I heard him ask Tess about the bull. Being the woman she is, she told him the whole story. Every now and then paw would chuckle lowly and say "You don't mean it?" or "Did he really do that?" After the talk kind of died down and the room had been quiet a spell, I heard paw say, "The boy's got it in him alright. I've seen it. When he gets like that, the feller bringin trouble better look out."

The third time I had that feeling come over me was well into my seventeenth year. I was coming back to the house from checking on the stock. Tess was home doing some of her chores. Paw was off on another one of his wanderings. I remember riding up out of the river bottom and coming to the house through the thicket that flanked the north side of the yard.

As I walked my horse through the thicket, I heard some loud voices and laughter from the house. Knowing Tess was supposed to be there by herself, I eased out of the saddle and ground-hitched my horse. Taking my rifle in hand, I moved slowly to the edge of the thicket. The first thing I saw was three horses standing at the back side of the house. Beyond them stood three rough looking men. They were about ten paces from Tess and had her boxed in up against the house. She had a large butcher knife in her hand and she was telling them what she would do if they came any closer. They were having fun with my sister. They were telling her what they were about to do with her. I had never heard a man talk like that around my sister. I should have left her alone with them cause they didn't know what kind of she-wolf they had cornered.

Before I knew it that storm feeling rose up in me. I walked out of the thicket and slipped right up behind them. They were so caught up with Tess that they didn't hear me coming. Without warning I stepped around the big man on my left and hit him square in the mouth with the butt of my rifle. He fell like he had been hit in the head with a pole-axe. I dropped my rifle muzzle on the man on the far side and shot him in the shoulder as he went for his gun. The man in the middle was stunned and found himself looking down my rifle barrel. I walked around in front of him with a hope he would give me a reason to shoot. Tess started talking a mile a minute, telling me how she was cleaning a chicken on the old table out back when they surprised her.

The man I hit was out cold. I could count four teeth on the ground and blood was spilling out his mouth. The feller I shot was crumpled on the ground, crying in pain while the shock of that bullet started to tell on him. The third man stood quiet and looked at me with a fearsome mean look. I had him unbuckle his gun belt and throw it at my feet. I then took the guns of the other two and waited for the man I had hit to come around.

When he came to, I sent Tess in the house. I then had them strip down naked. It was a pitiful sight—one bleeding from his shoulder—one bleeding through a busted up mouth—and one standing there trying to look mean.

"My name is Bud Haddok," I spoke. "This is the Rocking H ranch. It's on the Brazos river and it's easy to find. I'm going to take your horses, your guns, gear, and clothes. If you are real careful, I'm going to let you keep your lives. If you decide you want to come back and claim your things, then come right on. I will kill you."

I then walked right up to the feller who as yet had been

untouched and rammed the barrel of my rifle into his gut. Holding it with my left hand I slipped my knife out of my belt. His eyes widened and settled on the blade of that knife. I stuck the point into his face in front of his left ear. I pulled it down to the corner of his mouth and sliced the flesh like a piece of beef. He winced, but did not move. I looked him in the eyes and saw the meaness leave and quit slip in. I spoke so softly that the other two could hardly hear.

"I hope you come back."

I walked back a few steps and said, "I'm gonna give you boys a break you would not have given my sister. I'm gonna count to ten, and then I'm starting to shoot." When I hit one they lit out toward the river a fretful sight, bare-assed and bleeding. I let them get nearly to the river before I let one fly over their heads. I heard them yell and then a splash as they started to pull water.

I added three horses and saddles to the ranch that day. It was also when I got my first pistol. It was a navy colt that the man I cut had been wearing. The other two pistols and two good rifles I put in the house. The three had seven dollars between them. I stuffed that into my pocket. I burned their clothes.

They never came back. I knew they wouldn't. When paw came home, he tried to get the story out of me and again had to settle on hearing it from Tess. He cornered me later and said, "Bud, watch your back. You've made yourself three enemies for life."

I thought for a minute, and said, "No paw, I think I made myself three friends."

He laughed and said, "Well—I guess so."

The last time I showed that side of me was about two weeks back. I had ridden into a little two-bit town that went by the name of Caution. I laughed when I saw the name and wondered how it might have come by it. It consisted of a main street lined by buildings thrown up in a hurry. Signs showed a couple of saloons, a general store, a cafe, and two places where you could get a bath and rent a bed.

I put my horses and some of my gear in the livery stable and made my way to the general store. I bought a new pair of socks, some britches, and a new shirt. I then went to one of the places where I could get a good bath. I soaked away a lot of the dirt and soreness of weeks on the trail. Then I rented me one of the beds. It was in a room that had four beds and the gent told me when I paid him that I would have to share the room.

It was gettin on late in the evening when I walked into the cafe to get me a good meal before turning in. The cafe was about half full of folks who were talking and enjoying their food. It seemed like a quiet and peaceable crowd. I wondered again about where the town got its name. I ordered me a meal of beefsteak, potatoes, and homemade bread. I topped it off with some berry pie. The coffee was good and I set for awhile just enjoying the sound of people talking.

When I got sleepy I went back to my bed and turned in. The other beds were empty. I blew out the lamp and drifted off to sleep. Wanting to live up to the warning in the town's name, I had put my knife under the blanket with me.

I heard them before the door swung open. I could tell by the sound of their laughing and cussin that they were pretty well drunk. When the light from the lamp outside spilled into the room, I could make out three or four bodies gathered around the door.

One of them said, "Git up feller. You got Bill's bed."

I Just laid there quiet like.

"Git up," the voice yelled, "or we'll throw you out."

I replied, "I paid for this bed and I'm gonna sleep in it—or nobody's gonna sleep in it."

They piled into the room and commenced to wrap me up in the blanket to toss me out. That feeling started rising up in me again and I cut my way out of the blanket and through most of their clothes.

One yelled, "He cut me." Another screamed like he had run up on a mountain lion. By that time I was on my feet with them gents backed against the wall, yelling over their spilled blood. I had cut one across the seat of his pants, one across the arm, one down his back, and the last one down the left leg. They could see the gleam of that old knife and they didn't want any more. I guess I was lucky they didn't start shooting in that little room. By the time they could have thought about it, it was over for them. Their pain was horrible.

With my rifle in hand I spoke, "You boys could have had a good night if you had left me alone. My name is Bud Haddok. I'm taking my gear and leaving. If you follow me, I'll kill you."

In a couple of swift moves I gathered my gear and left them crying in pain. I made it to the livery, threw my saddle and gear on the horses, and left town out the back street.

Looking back on these three set-to's, I have come to the notion that when I get pushed, another man steps into my body. The way I acted during them times is a puzzle to me. I never tried to cause no man trouble. But here I am, with trouble surely on my backtrail. I'm getting tired of looking over my shoulder. If whoever is back there don't show up tonight, I just might have to go back and invite them on in.

The fire was down to a few glowing embers and I was awake from my first round of sleep. On the trail by myself, I had settled in to sleeping about an hour, waking up and listening for a few minutes, and then drifting back to sleep. I had done it so often that it was now natural.

I looked at my horses and they showed no sign of uneasiness. The spot where I slept was dark, but I could make them out in the shadows. My night vision was better than most. However, it was my sense of smell and my intuition that served me best. I breathed in the smell of the forest and there was no unusual scent. I heard nothing that was not the sound of the night—the wind gently blowing in the trees and occasionally a cone falling. But something down inside me told me that something or somebody was out there close by.

I slid out from under my blanket, taking my rifle with me, and eased about fifteen feet to my right. I dropped in behind a big old tree that had fallen back toward the bluff. I had cleaned the path to it of all deadfall before dark and had cleaned out the spot where I now lay of all that would make a racket. The tree was big enough to conceal my entire body. The way it had fallen it had stopped about a foot off the ground.

Getting there as quietly as I could, I now settled down to see what was causing me that prickly feeling on the back of my neck. With all my senses running full out, I began my wait. After about twenty minutes of nothing, I tried to tell myself that I was just imagining things. But I still could not convince myself.

After waiting a while longer I decided to do something crazy. A man's best weapon in these kind of situations is his patience. What I was about to do was against the patience odds. I lowered my head down to the ground and cupped my hands so my voice would come out from under the tree. I spoke softly, but it sounded like I was yelling when the sound of my voice broke the silence of the night.

"What are you waiting on?"

Almost immediately a voice came out of the darkness from the bluff above me. "I was trying to find you and I didn't want to get shot."

"Who are you?"

My name is Josh Spencer. I cut your trail a few days back. I was in Caution when you left out and I figured to ride with you if we are headed the same direction."

We were talking so low that our voices could not be heard fifty paces away.

"You bringin any trouble?"

"Not me," he said, "but you have three apaches that cut your trail about four days back. I been trailing the whole lot of you since then. I've been trying to get around them and let you know they are doggin you."

"I knew somebody was back there, but I didn't know who."

"I figured as much, seeing how you've been settling in at night."

It was then that I took a chance. "If you ain't bringin trouble, then you can move about twenty-five paces to your left and you'll find a cut down off the bluff. When you get down to this level, hang close to the bluff. When you come to my horses you'll find my gear about fifteen feet past them. You keep your hands in plain sight. If you try anything, I'll kill you on the spot. Where's your horse?"

"Back up the way about three hundred yards."

"Leave him for now and come on down."

When the last word came out of my mouth I was already moving. It was to a spot I had scouted out before dark behind some low rocks that had slipped off the bluff sometime in the past. I settled in there quietly so I could see him when he came out of the cut. He was pretty good. I didn't hear a sound and of a sudden he stepped out on my level. I could see his hands hanging down by his side and he held his rifle in one hand well up in front of the trigger guard. He walked as quiet as a cat. He was looking in the direction he had located my voice coming from. He moved past my horses and up to my gear laying by the embers of the fire. His back was to me. He stopped and asked, "Are you coming out?"

I spoke from behind him, "Put your rifle down on the ground and set down right where you're standing."

If I startled him, he didn't show it. He chuckled a bit under his breath as he lowered his rifle and set down. He said, "You must be part Indian."

I walked around him and set down across the fire with my rifle pointed right at his belly. I threw a couple of dry sticks on the coals and they flamed up a mite to reveal a straight looking unshaved face and a big man dressed in well worn buckskins. He had a colt tied down, a wide brim hat, and a winsome smile on his face.

It would be the first of many fires we would share over the next few years.

L ooking across the fire at Josh Spencer I began to size him up. "What caused you to lock onto my trail?"

"Well, I thought I might want to learn a little more about you so I could make up my mind as to whether or not I should steer clear of a crazy man or help a good man keep from gettin killed." He broke out in a big smile as he said it.

"What do you mean by that?"

"Before I heard your name in Caution, I had already heard about a young kid named Haddok who backed down old Cyrus Larkin and a bunch of his riders back in Texas. I also heard the talk bout three fellers who showed up at Larkin's Lazy L buck naked and ground up like sausage. It seems they was begging clothes and any kind of help in heading west. They told it that they had run into a kid named Haddok. When I heard the news about your knife work in Caution, to tell the truth, I kind of wanted to see you for myself. The truth is, son, you have already made a name for yourself and it seems you don't even know it."

"I don't want no name for myself. I didn't go looking for trouble. They brought it to me."

"If it will make you feel any better, that's how I read it. Most folks are saying how you hadn't killed anybody, even though you might have had a reason to do so. Especially, if what I heard about those men mistreating your sister is true."

We talked on a while and I learned he was also from the Tennessee mountains and had drifted to the plains of Texas a few years back. He was heading west with the dream of having his own cattle ranch some day. We relaxed around each other and talked about how dreams were driving a lot of people west. It was good to have somebody to talk to. Before we knew it the night had mostly slipped by. Finally, I asked him if he was serious about riding along with me.

He answered, "If you will have me. I maybe can cover your back along the way if you ever need it."

I built the fire up a bit, made coffee, and sliced a few pieces of cured pork into a skillet. We ate while we talked. I told him we would break camp and lead my horses up through the cut he had walked down. We would pick up his horse on the way out. It took us a few minutes to get my rig together and on the pack horse. Silently we walked up the cut and onto the bluff that led southeasterly from my camp. We would ride down later and head back west.

Before we left camp I built the fire up big and took a little time arranging it for my friends who were following me. A little after sun up the Indians slipped into the camp. They found the fire died down to ashes and the white man gone. The three warriors had been puzzled by this white man because it seemed everything he did had a purpose. They found his spot cleaned out behind the log and how he placed himself beneath the bluff. They knew, as good as they were at sneaking up, they never would have got to him without a warning. They also noticed that he brushed out his tracks around the campsite so they could not learn his habits.

But the thing that really got their attention was the cross fashioned out of sticks and arranged by the fire. A rock lay at the ends of each stick. Shining in the light at the base of the cross were three rifle shells. At the top was one empty shell.

They sat down by this strange arrangement and talked most of the morning away trying to find meaning to it. In the end, they decided it was bad medicine to follow such a man who obviously knew they were on his trail. They left everything untouched. Returning to their horses, they departed north toward their home. The strange man and his cross would be talked about around many campfires through the winter.

We rode down off the rim about two miles south of our campsite and followed a small stream cutting through the mountain. We traveled a good distance in the water. It was knee deep on our horses. When we came out of the stream, we chose an area of gravel and stepped our horses up on a rock shelve. We followed the rocks for a long time to avoid leaving any tracks.

The sun had been up for about three hours when we pulled up on an outcropping of rock that allowed us a eyeful of the area ahead of us. It also gave us an excellent view of our backtrail.

We had not spoken during the morning but I had taken to Josh real well. He rode light in the saddle and he let his horse do the work. He carried his rifle at the ready and I was pretty sure he could get his pistol into action quickly if need be. The thing that impressed me most was how he was aware of everything around him. His eyes and his ears were constantly alert. At times, when he was in the lead, he would pull up instantly and just listen. This was one of my own mannerisms when moving in unknown and dangerous situations. I began to think that he would be a good man to ride the river with.

Sitting there in a position to view both directions and allowing our horses to graze nearby, Josh broke the silence.

"I've got a hunch those indians are not following us."

"What makes you feel that way?"

"I don't rightly know, but I noticed what you left for them."

"My paw taught me indians were curious and a bit superstitious. I thought I might give them a little something to play with their heads. You can't ever tell, it may keep me from having to kill them."

"Have you ever killed anybody?"

"Nope! I never have had to."

"Do you think you could if you had to?"

"Yes! If somebody brings me trouble and killing is the only way to handle it, I could kill without giving it a thought. I don't start trouble and I'll steer clear of it if I can. But when trouble boxes me in, I don't cut it no slack."

We set there plenty long enough to see if anyone was on our backtrail. We saw or heard nothing. We were gathering our horses to ride on when I asked Josh, "Are you any good with that pistol?"

He grinned and said, "Some would say yes. Most folks who have seen me draw it ain't alive to talk one way or the other."

"I can shoot mine fairly well," I said, "but I've never had anybody to show me how to draw and shoot. Would you show me?"

"Sure!" he responded. "When we get to where there ain't nobody looking down our backs I'll teach you. You got a good looking pistol. Where did you get it?"

"Oh, a feller gave it to me a while back."

He laughed and asked, "Was it one of those men running around naked?"

"Yep! He's one of those I didn't have to kill."

We saddled up and rode out of there. We were two men who knew little of each other, but with a growing awareness that we would be able to count on each other. I was becoming proud to have Josh Spencer at my side.

We rode on west for the day. Then we swung north in the low hills and rode for the better part of two days. Late in the afternoon of the third day we rode right into a rainstorm. We moved back into the hills til we found a bluff with an overhang. We set up camp there to get out of the rain. There was plenty of room for the horses and some grass for them to graze. We built a fire, dried our clothes, and put on a pot of coffee. We had become sure that no one was on our backtrail. I had doubled back the day before and waited til dark just to make sure. Feeling no danger and in no hurry, we decided to wait out the storm right there.

After we had downed the coffee and some jerked beef, we settled down to talking. That was one of the things I enjoyed most about having Josh around. During the conversation, I asked Josh again,"Will you show me how to draw and shoot a pistol?"

"Well, I guess now is as good a time as any to get you started."

He started with my belt and holster. He showed me that it needed to hang just so the natural hang of my hand would ride next to the handle on the pistol. He also tied the holster to my leg so it would not flop up when I pulled the pistol out. He took a little grease and rubbed it into the inside leather of the holster. He told me to do that every day for a couple of weeks til the leather was broke in good. With that done, he showed me how to pull up til the barrel cleared the holster and then to continue that motion by pointing at a target.

"Unload it and repeat that slowly, pulling the trigger when you bring it on the target."

I picked me out a tree some fifteen paces away and started to pull and fire. I did that for the rest of the afternoon and would speed up my draw til it would throw me off. Then I would slow down and work my way back up again.

Josh watched and later said, "It comes natural to you boy. You'll be all right when you can do it without thinking. Let me tell you something about pistol fighting. It's not about drawing fast, but about shooting straight. I've seen a lot of men get killed who drew faster, but missed. You always remember that a man with a bullit in his leg can still shoot a fast draw man through the heart."

29

"I've always been able to shoot, but I've never had much of a chance with a pistol. For some reason paw never used one and he never let me have one."

"So, your paw never did set much in store for pistol shooting, heh?" I noticed a bit of a smile on his face when he said it, but I didn't know why. He came back with this, "Just always remember, it's not the draw, but the shot that will make the difference. Make up your mind you will probably get hit, but that you also will kill the feller you are drawing against. Now you just work on drawing, pointing that barrel at your target, and pulling the trigger. After a while, we'll load her up and do some shooting."

The rain drug on for three days and most of that time I spent getting used to the feel of my pistol coming out of the holster and being a part of my hand. I also rubbed the inside of my holster with grease each day and the leather was getting as slick as glass. Along in the second day Josh told me to pick another target to go with my first and to practice going for two. He said that my judgement would have to come into play in a real fight when deciding which one to shoot first. He moved me around so my body would present the least target and made me do it over and over again. I was loving it and felt like I was doing pretty good.

"Am I fast enough to stay alive?" I asked him.

He walked up beside me and in a blur his hand flew up like lightning and he fired a round heart high into the tree I was using as a target. Just as quickly he had that pistol riding back in his holster. He looked at me and said, "I'm good, but there are those better than me. I know one that you couldn't pay me enough to draw against."

"Who?" I asked.

30

"I'll point him out to you if we ever cross his trail." He smiled again and walked away.

I knew then I had work to do. If Josh was slower than some, then I was slower than most. I went back to drawing and pulling the trigger.

The rain finally passed over in the evening of the third day. We headed on north at daybreak. We both knew that it wouldn't be long before real cold weather set in and we needed to find us a place to wait it out. As we rode down out of the hills we started noticing cattle carrying a Diamond brand. We reckoned that we must be coming up on a ranch. Late in the afternoon we topped out on a rise and saw the ranch off across a beautiful valley. We rode on toward it and pulled up when a group of six riders came out to meet us. From where we set the ranch looked to be a fair sized spread. The ranch house, barn, bunk house, and corrals were in good shape. When the riders got to where we were, they pulled up with their rifles casually, but purposefully, pointed in our direction.

A stout looking man with a little grey in his black hair spoke, "What can we do for you fellows?"

I replied, "I'm Reed Haddok and this here is Josh Spencer. We are out of the Brazos river country in Texas on our way west. We were hoping to find somebody who needed a couple of hands that would allow us a place to work through the winter."

The same feller asked, "You are not from around here?"

31

"No sir!" I said. "We've been on the trail for a while. We both have worked cattle and there ain't nothing about ranching we can't do."

"You'll have to pardon this kind of welcome. My name is Clint Forbes and I own the Diamond ranch. The big fellow here is Gus Trapp, my foreman."

He pointed to a man I guessed would stand six feet four and weigh about two-hundred and forty-five pounds. He looked to be in his early forties and I figured him quickly as one tough man. Mr. Forbes didn't introduce the rest of the men, but they all looked to be better than average.

"We have had some trouble of late," Forbes said, "and we have been a little careful with strangers."

Josh spoke up, "Mr Forbes, we need work and a place to hole up for winter. If you need us, your trouble will be our trouble, because we both will ride for the brand."

"Then why don't you come on to the house and we will talk about it over supper."

We all rode on to the ranch and tied our horses at the corral.

Forbes said, "You men can wash up out by the well and come on into the house. Supper is probably ready."

We washed as much of the trail dirt off as we could and made our way to the house, dusting our shirts and britches as we walked. When we entered the house the smell was like heaven. There was a big room full of chairs around a huge fireplace off to our left. There were two closed doors in a hallway to our right. At the end of the hallway a large table set with plates and food was calling our names.

Forbes came out of the fireplace room and led us down the

hallway to the food. The house was strong and well kept. As we walked into the eating room my mind was set on the beef and potatoes along with the bowl of gravy and big loaves of fresh baked bread. I was so caught up with the food that I almost missed seeing the most beautiful woman I had ever laid eyes on. There she stood with a big pitcher of milk and wearing a white dress that matched the milk. She had black hair and big black eyes. She was well put together and I found myself just standing there gawking.

Forbes introduced her. "Reed Haddok and Josh Spencer, meet my daughter Samantha."

I said, embarrased like, "Howdy, Samantha."

Josh said, "Howdy!"

She smiled real big and said, "Hello. You can call me Sam."

We pulled out chairs and set around the table, Mr. Forbes, Sam, Gus Trapp, Josh, and me. We set in to eating and small talk and I aimed to do two things. I wanted to eat as much as I could and watch that pretty woman as long as I could. Just listening, I could tell that she and her father had a lot of book learning. They talked of travel and it was interesting to hear about Boston and Charlotte and places I had never seen. I pretty much kept my mouth shut except for eating. I wondered what a woman like Sam found to keep her happy around a ranch way out here in the middle of nowhere. After supper the men moved to the setting room and Mr. Forbes started talking about the ranch.

"The Diamond gets its name from the boundries of the land."

He laid out a map and sure enough, the ranch was a big old diamond shaped piece of land that covered a hunk of territory. He also told us that he grazed some open land close to his.

"From this point to this point, it's a little over ninety miles," he said. "All in all, we probably have over five thousand head of cattle. I drive beef to the market in the late summer. I keep the best of the young stuff and sell off the rest, along with any of my older stock that I feel like is about passed their prime. The ranch is very productive and I take good care of my hands. I have thirty-two men on the place and some of them have been with me for a long time. They are all good men who can handle themselves in any kind of spot. With a ranch this size, we all stay kind of spread out. Most of the time there's no more than eight to ten of them here at a time"

He talked on and I got the idea he was good at ranching and leading men. After a while, he got to where I figured he had been heading all the time.

"I could use you men if you really want a job for the winter. But I don't think I could hire you without telling you what you might be up against. There's some folks up north of Prescott that's throwing a wide loop. We've had some of our cattle rustled and we've had some hay that we gathered against the winter burned. We build dams to hold run-off water from the mountains and some of those tanks have been salted. Two of my men have been wounded from ambush and some of my men have run into some hired guns while in town. These gunslingers tried to goad my men into a fight. My men will fight, but they are not gunfighters. What I'm telling you now is exactly the reason we rode out to meet you like we did. I must say that the way you both wear your pistols tied down still leaves me a little edgy. But I reckon you are who you say you are, and that you do need a job."

"Mr. Forbes," I answered, "I can't speak for Josh, but my gun

34

could never be hired. I need a job. If you hire me to herd cows and doing that causes me to have to use my brains, sweat, blood, gun, or whatever, I'll be a Diamond man as long as I'm taking Diamond money."

Josh added, with that grin spread across his face as if he was proud of what I had said, "That goes double for me!

"In that case, you are hired. I've got a line shack up in the mountains in this valley." Forbes spoke while pointing to a spot on the map that showed a wide circle of mountains surrounding a natural bowl. "It is already holding about nine hundred head of our best stock. We have laid in hay back against the bluff and the water runs there the year through. The mountains shield the wind and the snow never gets real deep in the valley. However, the trail up there gets blocked in about three weeks from now. I want you two to pack enough supplies to last for at least four months and go up there and take care of my cows. When winter breaks and the trail is open, you can start them back down. All it takes is starting them. They'll come right on down to fresh grass. Do you want the job?"

We looked at each other and when Josh nodded, I said, "You've hired yourself two men."

"Good! Gus will show you where to bunk for the night and he'll help you get your gear ready in the morning. Be sure to pick up a winter coat before you leave. We've got plenty in the bunkhouse. Also, if I was you, I'd spend the first few days before winter sets in getting the lay of the land up there and laying in plenty of firewood. It's a lot better to do both before you need it."

We said goodnight and followed Gus to a large bunkhouse about a hundred paces from the house. Once inside, we found us a empty bunk and claimed it. After stripping our gear from the horses and feeding them, we went back to get some sleep. It was the first real bed I had seen in a while. I had my mind on a winter of hard work and a beautiful blackhaired woman as I lay there waiting on sleep to come. As I drifted off to sleep, the woman won out.

We were already up when morning broke. We had our breakfast in a big room off the side of the bunkhouse. Gus told us to pick a pair of packhorses to go along with mine. We got busy putting together the provisions we would need for the winter. Gus also told us we could probably kill some game for meat while up there, but we had better take enough cured meat in case game was scarce. We both picked out a winter coat, some blankets, and some longjohns. After we had it all loaded, Gus told us that he was going to ride with us to the canyon.

As we worked around getting ready, I kept looking toward the ranchhouse. I didn't see any sign of a beautiful blackhaired woman. When we saddled up, Gus kept waiting for something and I was about to ask what we were waiting for when a rider swung out of the barn on a big red gelding. It took me back for a minute when I realized it was Sam. She had her hat pulled down almost to her eyes and had every look of a cowhand, all the way to the pistol strapped around her waist.

She smiled and said, "Good morning men," as she rode up and Gus turned to lead us toward the mountains.

I watched her set that horse and she was at home on him. He was full of spirit and she handled him like a baby. I looked at Josh and he kind of grinned and rode on up in front of me.

We rode at a steady clip for about two hours and then we began to climb. We were getting into timber but the trail was wide at this point and showed the signs of cattle traveling in the same direction we were going. I rode with my normal alertness as we now slowly moved higher and higher. We stopped to let the horses blow a little and then moved on.

I heard the sound of cattle bawling just as we rounded a big boulder and found myself facing two men who had their pistols out and already had the drop on Gus and Sam. Josh and I rode up beside them. I had the hammer eared back on my rifle and it was pointing right at one of the rider's belly. It was hardly a thing a person would notice since my rifle lay casually across the saddle horn. I looked around and quickly determined that they must be bringing some Diamond cattle off the mountain. The fact that they surprised us must have been because they had someone riding in front of them who could ride with a warning. In that case, someone else was laying up in the rocks with a bead on us.

Gus spoke,"What are you doing on Diamond land?"

The man my rifle was pointed at said, "We're borrowing some cows. Now if you don't want to get this lady hurt, you drop your guns right now."

Gus and Sam pulled their pistols carefully and dropped them to the ground. They both had rifles, but they still rode in the saddle slings. Josh didn't move and neither did I. If a man gives up his gun, he's at the mercy of the man who has one. I never planned on being at any man's mercy.

The man doing the talking looked at us and said, "Drop your guns."

I spoke calmly and quietly, "I been settin here trying to decide whether or not to kill you. Now, don't get me wrong. I don't want the lady to get hurt. But I don't reckon giving up my gun is the way to keep that from happening, seeing as how I got it pointed right at your gut with the hammer back and a trigger that can't stand much more pressure than what I'm putting to it. I know you got somebody laid up there with a gun on us and I know if we start shooting, a lot of us will get hit. The thing I want you to know is that you are going to die for certain. I'm going to blow a hole clean through you and there's no way you can keep it from happening. Unless, of course, you want to call that man down here and the lot of you want to take up another job. I don't know who's paying you, but I'd bet the wages ain't enough to die for."

I set there and watched the sweat break out on his face. I looked into his eyes and saw it when doubt and fear walked in. He was about to quit. I helped him on a little by saying, "I'm gettin a little tired of holding my trigger finger back. I really don't care what you decide, but you better do it quick."

Sweat was drippin off his nose. He lowered his pistol a mite and hollered, "Come on down Joe." In a minute or so, the third man rode up and he had his pistol holstered. He was sure that his buddies were in control.

I spoke, "Now the three of you are going to make an important decision—whether to live or die. If you want to live, be real careful and drop your guns to the ground. If you want to die, then start shooting."

The last feller to arrive looked sick, like he had been invited to the wrong party. He looked at the other two for some kind of read and was startled when they gently lifted their pistols and dropped them to the ground. He followed suit. They chose to live.

"Gus, if you and Sam will start the cattle back up the mountain, me and Josh will tend to these gents."

Gus retrieved his and Sam's pistols and they moved out to start the cattle uphill. After they were gone we both dismounted and I ordered the three men to do the same. I walked in front of them and said, "Now, off with your clothes."

"Now look here," one of them argued.

"I'm gonna try to keep from looking," I said with a chuckle. "We could rightly hang the three of you with no questions asked. We ought to shoot you. But I'm gonna give you your lives with the hope you've learned something today. Now, get your clothes off or I'll cut them off."

They undressed down to the pitiful sight they were. When they were naked, I said, "Now me and Josh are going to spend the winter in a line shack up in the canyon. If you boys are lucky, you can go back and get you a new outfit before the snow sets in. You can then come back up here and settle the score with us if you want to. If you don't have enough time, then you can wait til after winter and you'll find us riding off the mountain down this same trail. But I want you to know that if I ever see any of you again, I'm going to kill you on the spot. The one place you don't want to be is on Diamond land or in my gunsights."

The feller who had been laid up in the rocks said, "You talk mighty big with that gun in your hand and me without one."

I moved closer to him and poked my rifle barrel right up against his naked belly. I slipped my knife out with my left hand and dry shaved half of the beard on the right side of his face. I got a little skin with the hair. I looked deep into his eyes and told him, "The only thing keeping you alive right now is the fact that I have a gun and you don't. Do you want me to give you one?"

Fear was all over his face and quit was bright in his eyes. The other two seemed to be pleading with their eyes for him to leave it alone.

"My name is Reed Haddok. I won't be hard to find. I'll be on the Diamond when you get ready to come looking. Now you fellers better start gettin off this mountain cause it gets kind of cold up here when the sun goes down."

They lit out of there without any encouragement and a awful sight they were. We stood and watched them til they disappeared, running down the mountain.

Josh glanced at me and said, "Boy, you don't ever have to buy no new clothes. You are always taking somebody elses."

"There's nothing like gettin back to nature to humble a man and make him do some serious thinking about where he's going with his life."

"Well, whatever. I know one thing. It's a pleasure to watch you work. I was pretty sure they had the drop on us and you made them think we had them."

"That don't always work. If a man wants to live, you can

bargain with him about his life. If he don't care one way or the other, then you don't talk—you shoot."

We gathered up their gear and horses and headed on up the mountain. Gus and Sam were driving the cattle out into the canyon when we caught up to them. When we made it to the shack, Gus said, "You could have gotten Sam or all of us killed back there."

I said, "I'm pretty sure none of us would be alive right now if we had given in. The truth is, we are alive, the cattle are safe, and Mr. Forbes has three new horses, saddles, rifles, pistols, and a whole pile of used clothes."

Sam was laughing with the thought of those men naked back down the trail and she said, "Gus, we might see if we can cut their trail as we head back. Daddy is going to get a kick out of hearing about this."

We unloaded, rustled up some grub and ate. We then said so-long to Gus and the blackhaired woman who was spending a lot of time on my mind.

After they left, Josh looked across at me and said, "Four months is a long time to spend holed up with you. I might have to build me a cabin of my own."

I laughed and punched him on the shoulder in a kidding way and said, "Fine! I'll help you."

41

We spent the first day getting settled into our winter house and riding out the entire canyon. It contained about four hundred acres of rich meadow that was surrounded with trees that ran back against the bluffs. The bluffs jumped up one hundred and fifty feet in places and at no place seemed to drop under fifty feet.

It was impossible for a rider to get into the canyon except by the trail we came up. At the mouth of the canyon the trail cut through the rocks and was about fifty paces across. The cabin set back against the opposite side of the canyon from the entrance and offered a full view of anyone who might come in. The cattle were in good shape and the hay laid up against the bluffs was a plenty. As it started to get dark on our first night, I rode back to the entrance and down the trail a spell to set and listen.

When I got back Josh had some bacon and beans cooked. We ate a quiet supper while looking out over the moonlit valley filled with cattle. It was a beautiful sight. We decided that until the snow blocked us in we probably ought to sleep in shifts with one of us awake at all times. We didn't want to get surprised. I slept first and Josh woke me a little after midnight. I drank coffee and huddled in a blanket on the porch of the cabin the rest of the night.

After I woke Josh in the hour after daybreak, I told him I thought one of us ought to ride the canyon rim just to make sure we hadn't missed a place where we might get surprised. He said he would get started on the firewood if I wanted to ride it out.

So, after some breakfast, I saddled up and rode out of the

canyon. I rode up the mountain toward the bluff that ringed the canyon. When I got there I rode right up against the bluff as close as I could get and stopped a few times to walk up and check some places. It was really a box canyon. I wasn't sure such a place actually existed up til now. I figured there wasn't a canyon I couldn't get out of. Well, if a feller got out of here, he would have to be part mountain goat. After I rode around the canyon close to the bluff I retraced my route back from the rim about three hundred paces. I was looking for any sign that would indicate travel up there or any vantage point. The cabin was never in view because of the trees and only at a few places could a man see much of the meadow.

I saw a few game trails, but they were all leading around the canyon. I thought, as I studied the area, that it was an ideal place to hole up. The best chance to kill a deer in the winter would be the meadow in the canyon or where the small stream flowing out of the canyon reached the entrance. I had seen deer tracks along with those of other small game there.

It was the middle of the afternoon when I got back to the cabin. Josh had brought up a good bit of firewood, but we knew we would probably need all we could get.

When I swung down, Josh asked, "Well, how does it look?"

"If anybody comes to visit or shoot, they are going to have to come through the front door. That'll make it a lot better for us, won't it?"

"Yes! Unless we ever need a back door to get out." He laughed when he said it.

After about a week of gathering firewood and getting settled into a routine, we developed a love and appreciation for this place.

At night we would talk about how it wouldn't be a bad place to stay all the time. It was the eighth day when the first snow fell. It snowed for the better part of the day and tapered off about dark. That meadow sure looked bright when the moon hit it. It was almost like daylight. The snow held off for another three days and then set in. We didn't have a day without some snow for the rest of the winter.

I felt a little better when the trail up to the canyon was completely closed. We could focus on the cattle and sleep at night without worrying about somebody sneaking up on us. We killed two deer during the first week of snow. We enjoyed the fresh meat. It was plenty cold to keep the meat from ruining so we didn't have to rely on all the cured meat til later in the winter.

I spent a lot of time working on the fast draw of my pistol. I got to where it was natural. I practiced drawing and actually shooting at targets. The shooting was no problem. I could always shoot. The pistol was different from my rifle, but my hand and eyes worked together pretty good. I got to where I could hit what I was shooting at. Since the day I had seen Josh draw and fire, I had not made the slightest hint toward my progress. I always worked on it when he was not around. One afternoon Josh rode back from checking on the cattle and saw me practicing. I stopped and we both walked into the cabin. When the door closed and he came out of his coat, he walked around in front of me.

"Well Bud, let's see how good you are."

He suggested that we both unload our pistols and have a contest.

"I guess I need to find out if I've moved up to good," I said.

We unloaded and faced each other. He held one of the pistol

shells in his left hand. He spoke, "Draw when you hear it hit the floor."

"Okay!"

I figured he would have the edge because he would know when he dropped it. I stood calmly waiting for the sound. When I heard it I pulled in one swift motion and pointed my pistol at him. He hardly cleared the leather when he heard the click of my hammer fall. He grinned kind of sheepishly.

"I guess I'll have to add another name to that list you couldn't pay me to draw against."

We loaded them back up and from that moment I knew that if it ever came to it, I could stand against another man and hold my own.

"You never did tell me who the man was that topped your list of fast draws."

"Nope! I never did. He goes by the name of Doc. He's a gun for hire. His specialty is cleaning up towns that have been taken over by crooks and gunslingers. He probably has twelve to fifteen towns to his credit. He's a good man and he's definitely law and order. If he was an outlaw, everybody would be looking for a place to hide."

"I'd like to meet him. He sounds like an interesting feller."

"I've rode with him and call him friend. Maybe I can introduce you to him some day."

"Maybe so," I said as I started to stir us up some grub.

The winter felt long. The mountains and trees blocked the wind and we survived well. The cattle stayed back in the trees at night and rustled the grass they could get to in the meadow during the day. The hay held up good and the cattle actually put on weight.

Me and Josh molded into quite a team. We could almost read

each other's mind. We enjoyed each other's company. He became the first person outside my family that I trusted completely. It was good to have that kind of friend.

Winter broke and the trail finally opened. We headed the cattle out of the canyon and started them down. Mr. Forbes was right. All we had to do was point them down the mountain and they did the rest.

Me and Josh were a sight to look at. We had gotten pretty wooly during the winter. We couldn't wait for a chance to soak and shave. Our hair had grown down over our necks and the cold had toughened our skin.

As we followed the cattle down we rode light in the saddle. We expected to find trouble at every turn of the trail. There was no sign of the men we had sent packing when we came up. There was no sign of anyone as a matter of fact.

The cattle scattered out in the low hills and started grazing. The range was covered with fresh young grass and they took to it like a cat to milk. We rode on through and headed for the ranch. When we rode in we were welcomed by what seemed to be all the cowhands on the ranch. We were lucky the men who were there when we hired on were present. The whole lot was angry and fired up. We went into the bunkhouse and they filled us in on what had happened the past two weeks.

Some of the men had gone into Prescott. The town was about a day's ride from the ranch. While there, they had been goaded into a gunfight. One of the cowhands had been killed and another wounded. The wounded man had been left in town in the care of the doctor. Mr. Forbes and five of his men had ridden into town to check on him and to talk to the sheriff. On the way back Mr. Forbes was shot from ambush and was laid up at the house with a bad wound in his side. Along with all this, some cattle had been rustled. All the men had been called in to the ranch and were guarding it. Gus and a few men were away at the time checking on some cattle. As they talked on about the situation, it was easy to tell that the men were pretty worked up and ready to go do something about it. The trouble was, they didn't know who was behind all the shooting and stealing.

We went on up to the house and knocked on the door. Sam opened the door and she looked as pretty as ever, even though she looked tired and worried. She was happy to see us and started in telling us again all that had happened. She filled in some places the men outside had not hit on. She told us her father was going to be all right, but he was going to need a lot of rest. The bullet that hit him had been fired from above him and had entered high under his right arm and had come out just above his belt on his back side. The doctor had said the bullet had not broken any bones, but it tore a big hole. He had lost a lot of blood. We asked if we could talk with him and she left to check and see if he was awake. She came right back and led us to his room. He was propped up a little on pillows and managed a weak smile when we walked up beside the bed.

"How'd you men make it through the winter?"

"We did fine and brought the cattle down in good shape," Josh responded.

"Sam told me about your little set-to on the way up. I wish I could have been there to see it."

"I hope what happened up there didn't bring you this trouble," I added.

"No, son—this trouble has been coming long before you men got here. I just wish I knew who was behind it and what they are after."

We talked on a bit and he said the only talk he had heard was about a man named Beecham who had bought a big spread north of Prescott called the Bar J. The word was that he then pressured some smaller ranches to sell to him and that he had more men on his payroll than it took to run the ranch. The sheriff had told him, while he was in town checking on his wounded man, that he thought the men involved in the gunfight were Bar J men, although he had no proof. Witnesses had testified that it was a fair fight and no charges had been filed. Beecham no doubt was a powerful man because his money had already won over much of the business community, notably the banker, Frank Grimes, and a Moss Henderson, who runs the general store.

Forbes added, "I believe the sheriff is a good man, but he may not have much support from the rest of the town."

He then told us that Gus would pay our wages and we were free to leave whenever we wanted to. He knew that we had only hired on for the winter. He thanked us for the good job we had done.

Me and Josh stood there looking at each other for a little while and I answered for both of us. "Mr Forbes, we ain't in much a

48

hurry. If you don't mind, we'll stay on a spell til you get back on your feet."

Josh joined in, "You can count on us to do what we can to help."

"Thanks! I kind of hoped you would stay a while longer. I'm worried about Samantha. I would like it if you kept a special eye on her."

"You can count on that too," Josh said.

I'm going to tell Gus to let you both have a free rein in moving around the ranch. See what you can find out and let me know what we are up against."

We told him we would and left his room. On the way out, Sam met us in the hall and we told her of her father's wishes and that we were going to help.

"I don't think I need any help in taking care of myself, but it is good to know you are going to stay around."

We asked her to stay close to the ranch house for a few days until we could sort some things out. She agreed and we left to put our gear up. We also wanted a good bath and shave. While we were cleaning up, I told Josh that I thought I would take a couple of days and ride into Prescott and see what I could find out. I suggested that he check out the ranch and try to find out the route the outlaws were taking when they rustled the cattle. We also needed to learn any other patterns in their activity. He agreed and we decided to head out in the morning. During the night I thought about the ranch, Sam, and her father, and decided there was a definite attempt being made to run them off. The answers to who and why was what I was going to be after. I went to sleep with Sam's last words on my mind.

With daybreak and breakfast behind us, me and Josh had a talk with Gus. He had rode in during the night and had just returned to the bunkhouse after having breakfast up at the house with Mr. Forbes. The boss had told him about our staying on and that he wanted us to be free to check out some things. Gus seemed pleased that we were staying. He paid us our winter wages. Sixty dollars was a lot of money for me. I told him I was going into Prescott and that Josh was going to do some checking around the ranch. He gave me some advice about going into town.

"Avoid trouble if you can, because they have been stacking the deck with our men. They will try to get you into a situation where you have to fight and you will be outnumbered."

After I thanked him, he pointed Josh in the direction north where they had been losing cattle. We said our farewells and rode out.

As I headed toward Prescott I rode away from the wagon ruts of the road and held close to as much cover as possible. If someone was watching the road, I sure as heck wasn't going to give him an easy target. I rode careful and thought as I rode. They wouldn't know me in town unless one of the three men I met on the mountain happened to be around. My horse didn't carry a Diamond brand. If I came into town away from the normal trail, I might go unnoticed long enough to find out a few things.

I enjoyed the ride and saw no riders. When I topped out on a ridge and saw the town, it was getting late in the afternoon. I circled the town and came in from the opposite direction of the Diamond. It was dusky dark when I rode in and headed for the livery.

Prescott was a big town by my standards. It sat on a plateau high up from the low land of Arizona. It was close to a army garrison at Fort Whipple. Mr. Forbes had told me that it was the center for most of the trade in the territory. I had noticed a school building and two churches as I rode in. There was a bunch of houses away from the main street. Main street was lined with stores, a bank, and a doctor's office. I reckoned that the saloons and night life was on down the street because when I pulled into the livery I could see the lights and hear the music and laughter coming from that direction.

The hostler met me as I was getting off my horse and I asked him to feed him some grain and stable him for the night.

"My name's Bussler," he said, "but everybody calls me Bob." He was a big man with a friendly smile.

"My name's Haddok," I told him.

"How long you planning to be in town?"

"A couple days at the most." I could tell he was trying to find out all he could about me.

"Well, be careful. We've got a rough sort in town of late and there have been a bunch of shootings."

"What's it all about?"

"I really don't know. About six months ago we started having some gunslinger types drifting into town. We've had one or two in the past but they never stayed for long. This bunch has grown and now I reckon there must be about fifteen of them."

"Are they working together or fighting each other?"

"At first I thought it was coincidence. But now I'm pretty sure they all know each other. They hang around together and they are good at goading a man into a fight. They killed a cowhand off the Diamond a couple weeks back and another is laid up over at the doctor's office all shot up. Those Diamond men didn't want to fight, but the gunslingers wouldn't give'em no way out."

"Do you have any names to go with the gunslingers?"

"I think the ring leader is a man who goes by the name of Sledge. There's a half breed they call Slay. The two who did the shooting with the Diamond men are Tuggles and Hape. They have been the cock of the walk around town since then. I may be talking too much. I been noticing how you wear your pistol tied down. I hope you ain't one of them. If you are, I guess I'm in big trouble."

"Bob, my gun ain't for hire. You don't have to worry about me. You take care of my horse. I appreciate you lettin me know what's going on in town. It always helps to know. If there's anything else you need to tell me, then do so. If you are asked about me or if anybody checks out my horse, we never had this conversation. I would like to know if someone has hired these men and brought them to Prescott or if they've come on their own?"

"The talk is that they work for Beecham and the Bar J. However, nobody's seen them together. We've noticed that the Bar J riders never have any trouble with them while everybody else who comes to town seems to."

"Who is this man Beecham?"

"He bought the Bar J a while back and come into town spreading money around like crazy. He's got half the folks in town and a lot of the ranchers beholding to him. All that money fogged up their thinking and now they can't hardly say anything against him. A lot of them ain't willing to admit that he's behind all this. But if I was a bettin man, I'd bet he's paying the gunslingers their wages."

"Well, point me toward a place where I can get something to eat and a place to sleep. I'll get out of your hair and let you get some work done."

"Fort Misery is the best eating in town. It's right up the street on the left. It's run by a woman we know as Virgin Mary. I don't know where she got her name. They also have rooms to rent reasonable."

"Thanks, friend. Keep your eyes and ears open for me. If I get into any trouble, I will not bring you into it."

"Young man, if you get into any trouble, you can come here. I got me a scatter gun that can stand up against a passel of gunslingers, and I don't take water from no man."

He smiled when he said it and I thought, he'll do to ride the river with.

"The Paradise is the saloon where they hang out, but you are liable to run into them anywhere."

"Thanks!" I spoke as I waved and walked up the board sidewalk. I held my rifle casually in my right hand, but I was ready for action.

I found Fort Misery and walked in. I took a table in the corner to the right of the door. I had a wall to my back. There were no windows. I had a full view of the room. A gent came from behind the counter and walked over to my table.

"What'll it be for you?" he asked.

"I want something to eat. What do you have tonight?"

"The venison stew is good. The pot roast is the best you'll ever eat. I can also fix you some eggs and steak."

"Bring the roast and plenty of coffee. I also need a room. Who do I see about that?"

"You're talking to him. The room is two bits a night. You can have the one on the right at the top of the stairs if you want it." He motioned to the stairs at the back of the cafe.

I told him I would take it. I settled in with the coffee and took the time to look over the cafe and the people who were eating. It was pretty full and to my knowledge nobody had even noticed me. I enjoyed the coffee and the man was right about the roast.

Just sitting there with my coffee, I thought back over what the hostler had told me. If Beecham and the Bar J was behind the trouble these folks were having, there had to be a reason. If he had money, then he could buy all the land he could work. Unless, of course, there was something else that would keep people from selling at what otherwise would be a good price. What could that be? My guess was that it was minerals of some sort. Gold and silver had a way of showing up in mountains of the kind around Prescott. Maybe he had stumbled onto something that was driving him to latch onto all the land he could before everyone else found out about it.

As I set there, my thoughts were interrupted when the door swung open and four men walked in and took a table to my front and two tables away. I casually looked them over. One man was short and stocky and did not carry a gun as I could see. Something told me down inside that he probably had one you could not see. The

54

other three appeared to be cowhands, although one of them carried his pistol like he could handle himself. He looked a cut above your average cowhand by the way his pistol was tied down, the way he looked around the room, and the casual way he kept his right hand free and close to his side. It was then I heard the name.

"What will it be today, Mr. Beecham?" the waiter said as he smiled and walked up to the table.

I'll take my usual," the stocky man replied, letting me put a name to the face. The other men ordered and they began to talk quietly among themselves. Two or three people walked over to their table and shook hands with Beecham like they were friends. I noticed others nodding in their direction and obviously talking about him. I did hear him call the man I had judged to be a gunman in cowhand clothes by the name of Sledge. I figured he was probably a bodyguard. Beecham looked the friendly type, but there was a side to him that made me think he could be one tough feller when he wanted to.

After a while, I eased my rifle out of the chair where it had been resting, paid for my supper and the room, and stood and walked across the room and up the stairs. My actions were calm and normal, but I felt that I was noticed as I did so. I'm sure they wondered who I might be.

The room was small, but the bed was good. A window looked out into the alley behind the cafe. There was no lock on the door. I could hear the sound of the people downstairs in the cafe. I propped the one chair in the room under the door handle and stretched out for a while. I had my pistol laying on my belly.

When I woke up it was quiet downstairs. I had slept for almost two hours. I got up and washed my face from the basin of water in my room. I then moved out into the hall and down the stairs.

The lights were low in the cafe and the man who waited on me earlier was cleaning up. I nodded to him as I walked through and out onto the walk. Looking up and down the street, I noticed no movement. The action was on up the street where the saloons were. There were a lot of horses tied up at the rails and, from the laughter and piano music, it sounded like they were having a good time.

I walked on in that direction and came to the Eagle saloon. I stood outside and looked the crowd over. I saw no one I recognized and the crowd seemed kind of quiet. Across the street was the Buffalo saloon and they sounded like they were having a party. Two buildings on up the street, on my side, was what I figured to be the Paradise. It had the biggest crowd according to the number of horses tied up. I walked on up that way and eased up to look in the window. There were four tables of card games going and a bar lined with men. Others were seated at tables. As I watched, a man left the bar and went through the back door. A little later he returned and I figured he had probably gone to the outhouse. If I could casually walk in from that direction, it might be possible to get in without attracting anybody's attention.

I backed up a few paces and stepped into the narrow lane between the two buildings. I moved down and then behind the saloon. I found the door, relaxed, and walked in. I set down at a table back close to the door where the light was dim. I looked the room over and became convinced that I had been unnoticed. I listened the best I could, but I couldn't pick up any conversation. I gathered that the crowd was a mix of cowhands, townspeople, and four gunslingers. The four were seated at a table on the far side. They were just talking and drinking whiskey. Their guns were tied down and they had that look about them.

I had been inside just a little while when the swinging doors flew open and two men walked in like they owned the place. The four gunslingers motioned them over and they fetched two more chairs for them. One of the men at the table yelled at the bartender, "Bring Tuggles and Hape a drink."

So, there they were. These gunslingers had set up two cowhands who rode for the man paying my wages. They were Diamond men. I'm a Diamond man. One of them is dead and one is laid up for no telling how long. They probably are the one's who ambushed my boss. I set there thinking about it and started to get mad. That feeling that causes me to do unlikely things started bouncing around in my head.

The table of gunslingers, now seating six men, had three rounds of drinks. Of a sudden, the four men who had been there all along pulled up and left. Tuggles and Hape continued to drink and talk. Finally, they got up and walked out.

I waited a minute and walked to the door to see them cross the street and enter an old building with a hotel sign out front. I stepped out onto the walk and moved into the shadows. A little later a lamp was lit in the room just above the front door. I could see their shadows against the shade. They were turning in.

I walked back to my room and waited for an hour. Then I returned to the hotel where Tuggles and Hape were bedded down. I eased in and up a narrow staircase. There was nobody in the lobby. I found the door to their room. I could hear them snoring. I tried the door and it was not locked. The hallway was dark so I just let the door swing open and I looked in to see them sound asleep. The whiskey they had downed had them sleeping like babies.

I eased inside the room and closed the door. I pulled my pistol and rapped one of them up side the head with the barrel. I then did the same for the other one. I took my knife and ripped a sheet and used some strips to tie their hands and feet. I also stuffed some into their mouths and tied it so they couldn't holler when they came to. With that done, I set back and waited for them to come around. There was enough light in the room to make them out. It didn't take long for them to start groaning and thrashing. They got real still when I spoke.

"You boys have picked the wrong road in life. I want to help you get back on the right one. You think you are good with your guns because you can outdraw some cowhand who knows nothing about a fast draw."

Their eyes were wide open and they were trying to make me out.

"I'm afraid you boys are in for trouble, because you'll run up against somebody who is good and you'll be dead. Now, I'm going to help save your life."

I walked over to one of them and rolled him over on his stomach. I grabbed his gun hand, and with one slice of my knife I cut his trigger finger off, right up where it joined the hand. He groaned and bucked around like a wild bronc. I turned to the other man and he was going crazy. But he wasn't going nowhere. I grabbed him, flipped him over, and gave him exactly the same help. They both were sobbing and crazy with pain. When I spoke again, they were paying me attention.

"My name is Haddok. I work for the Diamond. I ought to kill you both. I'm going to give you a chance to live. When you get loose, I want you to get up, gather your gear, and leave. Don't ever come back. If I see you again, I'm going to kill you on the spot. And believe me, I'm going to be looking for you. Do you understand me?"

There was real fear in their eyes. They both shook their heads wildly as if they were trying to convince me.

I opened the door, stepped into the dark hallway, and retraced my steps to my room. I washed the blood off my hands and my knife. Placing the chair back under the door latch, I stretched out for some sleep. It felt good to know that those two would never goad another unsuspecting man into a gunfight.

I woke up to the smell of coffee and food. By the sound of talking downstairs the breakfast crowd was already in the cafe.

I made my way on down and set down at the same table I took last night. The waiter brought me coffee without asking and I ordered up some eggs and steak. As I drank my coffee I checked out the people in the cafe. It was full and a buzzing with talk. As I listened I heard them mention the hotel and blood being everywhere. It seems nobody knew what had really happened. I also heard one man say the sheriff was checking it all out.

My breakfast came and I dug in. The food was good and I felt extra good for some reason. Maybe it was because I had been able to do a little something to settle the score for those two Diamond boys. When I had finished, I paid for my food and told the waiter I wouldn't be needing the room another night.

I walked out onto the street and headed back toward the doctor's office. The door was open and I stepped in to meet the old gentleman who took care of the sick folks in Prescott. I reached out my hand to him and said, "Hello! My name is Haddok and I work for Mr. Forbes at the Diamond."

He responded, "I'm Doc Summers. I suppose you have come to check on Jed Thomas."

"Yes sir! I thought I might see if he needed anything."

"Actually, I think he's in shape to go back to the ranch. Do you think you could come up with a buckboard so we could stretch him out and make him comfortable."

"You let me check with Bob over at the livery. If I can round one up, I'll head out of here about sundown and get him back to the ranch. Keep this under your hat because I don't want no trouble on the way with him in the shape he's in."

"I understand and I'll do it. We are having plenty of trouble and it appears somebody is settling some scores."

He went on to describe how he was woke up in the middle of the night by two men bleeding like stuck hogs. Each of them was minus a trigger finger.

"The word is that they were the same two men who gunned down the Diamond men. They had so much fear in their eyes when they showed up here that all they wanted was for me to patch them up so they could ride. They mumbled and groaned a lot and watched the front door like the devil himself would walk in at any minute. I patched them up the best I could and they lit out of here in a cloud of dust. I got the sheriff and he tracked their blood to a room in the hotel. He found it a mess and found their fingers just a laying on the floor. He's asking around now, but it appears nobody heard or seen anything. He talked to the friends of these two men early this morning and they rode out pronto. He may want to talk to you."

"I'll go see him when I leave here."

He showed me into a side room where Jed was stretched out in a bunk. He then returned to leave us alone.

"I'm Reed Haddok and I ride for the Diamond. I've been up in the mountains all winter."

"I know of you. We've all been waiting to meet the man who sent those rustlers packing naked as a new born babe. You didn't have anything to do with Tuggles and Hape losing their trigger fingers did you?"

I smiled and said, "A man ought to be mighty careful when he throws out a loop and starts running over people. Mighty careful! Especially if it is Diamond people they choose to run over. Those two men must not have been careful." I sort of winked at him and told him I would probably be back close to sundown to take him to the ranch.

I walked out of there and down the street to the sheriff's office.

When I walked in, I reached out my hand to the sheriff and said, "My name is Reed Haddok and I ride for the Diamond."

"Have a seat. I'm Sheriff Burgess."

"Doc Summers told me you had a busy night and that you might want to talk to me. I came into town planning to take Jed Thomas back to the ranch."

The sheriff went over the events of last night and early morning and finally said, "All I have is two dead fingers and no leads whatsoever. You don't know anything about all this do you?"

"Well, sheriff, it seems to me it's a simple case of two men who took a turn on the wrong road a while back and somebody has helped them to realize the error of their ways."

He looked me over pretty good and his eyes spent more time on my knife hanging on my pistol belt than anywhere else. Then he said, "That's the way I read it too. Son, I try to keep this town quiet and calm. We've had some gunslingers gathering here for a while. I'm not afraid of them, but the truth is, I'm outnumbered. They could take me in a minute if they decided to. They would do it just like they set up the Diamond men. Tuggles and Hape were two of them and I figure we are better off with them out of action. I've been afraid the lid is going to blow off this town and a lot of good people will get hurt, if not killed. The word is that some of the townfolk have sent a wire to hire a gunman to come run the gunslingers off. He goes by the name of Doc. He has a history of taming some tough towns. I hate to say it, but it would be a relief to have him here right now. I need some help."

"Sheriff, there are some men at the Diamond that would help you in a minute. You get word to us if you need us."

He thanked me and I left to make my way to the livery. When I stepped inside Bob was setting over by the window in a straight back chair. He had a smile on his face.

"Well, it seems like you had yourself a busy night."

"No! I got a good nights sleep. I did hear this morning that a couple of those gunslingers had a pretty rough night." I grinned back at him when I said it and understanding was written all over his face.

"I need a buckboard to get Jed back to the ranch. Do you have one I can rent?"

"I got one you can use as long as you need it."

"I want to pick him up from Doc Summers about sundown. Can you spare me a horse and get the buckboard over behind Doc Summers place about that time? If you can, then saddle and tie my horse behind the buckboard."

"I'll do it for you with pleasure, Son."

"Good. I think I'll spend the afternoon piled up in your hay over there. I'll be traveling all night so I'd better get me some sleep."

I walked over and slid into that haypile and dozed off to sleep. When I woke up it was getting late in the day and Bob had everything ready for me. I told him to give me about thirty minutes and I headed out the door and made my way to Doc Summers place. Doc had blankets ready for me. When Bob pulled up behind his office, we walked Jed out and stretched him out on the blankets. I covered him with a blanket and we made him as comfortable as possible. It was getting dark as I shook hands with Doc and Bob. I stepped up on the buckboard and pointed it up the alley toward the end of the street. I then worked my way out of town. If all went well, I should be back to the ranch about sunup.

L oyd Beecham was a hard man. He had grown up in New Orleans and had run away from home at the age of fourteen. He survived by finding odd jobs and running messages for the gangs that worked the waterfront. As he grew older he became more involved in illegal activity. His specialty was blackmail and extortion. He was physically a strong man and was above most when it came to fighting. He was not opposed to shooting a man, but he got a special thrill from whipping a man with his bare hands. Over the years he had killed four men in such a fashion.

At the age of forty-one he had left New Orleans just ahead of the law. There were several charges against him. Murder was the most serious. He left with a large sum of money he had been putting back for such a time. He made his way west and had spent two years in New Mexico. He learned through one of his contacts with a government minerals office about the tests on some ore taken from the mountains near Prescott, Arizona. He immediately put into motion a plan to acquire the property, listed as part of the Bar J ranch. The tests showed a high content of gold. He paid off the man in the minerals office and bought the ranch at a good price. He moved to the ranch and began his plan to own all the land in the area. His plan, up to now, had been working.

Beecham was pacing back and forth in front of the big fireplace in the ranch house at the Bar J. His face was a study of anger and frustration. He finally stopped and with lightning eyes looked straight at the man standing in the middle of the room.

"What's going on here, Sledge? You told me you brought in sixteen of the best men anywhere and now we are down to eleven. What bothers me is that we don't know who caused five of our men to jump and run."

"I ain't figured it out myself, Boss. Those boys who left out before winter set in showed up walking and wearing borrowed clothes. All they said was that they had run up on a man who was as cold as ice. He put the fear of death in them. They said you wasn't paying them enough to die. They didn't mind roughing up cowhands, but they got the notion that this man was hell on wheels."

"Who is he?"

"They said he told them his name was Haddok. I've never heard of him and I sure don't know how Forbes got hold of him."

"Do you think he's the one who got Tuggles and Hape?"

"Don't nobody seem to know. Tuggles and Hape didn't stay around to talk to nobody."

Beecham thought for a minute and then looked Sledge square in the eye. "We've come to far to back off now. Get that halfbreed of yours and a couple of your best men over to the Diamond. Tell them there will be a hundred dollars for each of them when I hear that Haddok is dead."

"Okay boss!"

Sledge walked across the room and out the door. When he got to the bunkhouse he told Slay to take Mead and Bolton and go to the Diamond ranch. He told them Beecham wanted Haddok dead.

Both Mead and Bolton had the classic look of gunfighters and they both had killed their share of men in gunfights. Slay was a weasel of a looking man who preferred to shoot a man from ambush. It had been Slay who shot Forbes from the rocks a few weeks back. When Sledge told them of the extra money tied to the killing, they couldn't leave fast enough. They didn't know what Haddok looked like so they would have to do some snooping around.

They rode hard and found a good place to watch the Diamond ranch house from a line of low hills that lay about a half mile from the house itself. The road to Prescott ran up against the hills so they had a good view of traffic to and from town. From their vantage point they could also watch the activities of the people around the ranch. They were on the down side of the slope facing the ranch in some low boulders shaded by trees. It would be near impossible to see them from below. It was a perfect spot.

It was about sundown by the time they got settled in. They had a little time to use their glass on the ranch, but could make out little in the fleeting light. They had no idea the man they were hunting was heading out of Prescott at that very minute and would ride just below them in a buckboard at sunup.

Mead was a mean man and thought little of killing. Eight men had died by his gun in shootouts. He had lost count of those he had shot in the back for money or those killed in holdups. He was a wanted man in New Mexico and other places.

Bolton was no different from Mead except he was about six years younger. They had been on the run together when they tied in with Sledge and went to work for Beecham as hired guns.

Slay was a different story. Born to a Seminole squaw and

fathered by an unknown white man, he had lived a life of struggle that stripped him of all moral consciousness. He could kill with knife or gun and never feel the slightest tinge of remorse. He had no friends, trusted no man, and could just as easily slit the throats of the two men hunkered down in the rocks with him as he could backshoot this man Haddok, who he hoped to kill before the next day was over. The three of them rolled up in blankets against the chill and waited out the night.

Haddok made pretty good time through the night and pulled up only twice to give Jed some water and to stretch his own legs. Jed seemed to be making the trip pretty good and only complained when they hit some rocky stretches in the road. Traveling under the cover of darkness was dangerous from the standpoint of missing a turn or hitting a hole. The up side was it reduced the danger of ambush considerably. As day began to break he picked up the pace. He saw the ranch off in the distance and settled the horse into a good trot, his mind beginning to think of hot coffee and Sam.

The sound of the buckboard stirred the three men up in the rocks and they rolled out to see the trailing dust as the buckboard passed below them. Slay put the glass on the buckboard and studied the driver. He made out a man laying in the back and figured him to be the Diamond man that had been laid up from the shootout. If the driver had been in town, he could be the man called Haddok. At least he could be the man who had sent Tuggles and Hape hightailing. He studied him the best he could. The brown flat topped hat was different enough to recognize. The trailing horse was a big black with two stockings of white on the front. He would be able to pick the man out later. The odds were good that this was Haddok and money in his pocket. He watched, along with the others, as the buckboard neared the ranch.

This could be his lucky day.

Two Diamond riders came out to meet us as we neared the ranch. It was obvious they had men guarding the ranch. They were thrilled to see Jed as they led us on into the yard. A crowd soon gathered around the buckboard. Sam was right in the middle of them. She looked mighty pretty early in the morning.

She said, "Help him into the house. I'll take care of him."

Josh sidled up to me and asked, "How was your trip? Did you learn anything?"

"Plenty! Let's go get some coffee and I'll tell you about it."

"I learned some things too. We'll put it all together and see what we can come up with."

We made our way to the eating room off the side of the bunkhouse and I dug into a pot of coffee and some biscuits and thick gravy. The coffee was good. After a spell of eating, I gave Josh the lowdown on the gunslingers, the sheriff, and Bob Bussler at the livery. I told him about the thinking of Bussler and the sheriff that the gunslingers were drawing their wages from Beecham at the Bar J. I also told him that the sheriff said some of the local people had wired for the gunfighter called Doc to come and run the gunslingers out of town.

"Well, what about that. Doc coming to Prescott. That'll be

something to see. I hope I'm around so I can watch." Josh mused over that possibility for a moment and then added, "Let me tell you what I found out."

He told me the rustlers had only been taking young unbranded cattle. He had found their trail and the carcasses of some branded cattle they had in their catch and had shot along the way. "They shot them and left them on Diamond land. They didn't want to be caught with them. I followed them clear through and right onto the Bar J. There's no way to catch them on those cows though, cause there is no brand to trace them back to the Diamond. I found where they are holding them. It's a little valley about three miles onto the Bar J. I injuned around enough to see that there are no Diamond brands on them young critters."

"How many people they got holding them?"

"I made out three, but they look like cowboys and not gunslingers. I also found something else mighty interesting. I found some heavy wagon ruts running back up into the mountains and I followed them and found a mining operation. They got about eight men working up there and it appears to be a pretty big setup."

"That's about what I figured. I knew there had to be a reason for Beecham to want all this land enough to try to weasel it away from the owners or to flat run them off."

"What do you think we ought to do?"

"I'm going to get some sleep and then we'll go fill Mr. Forbes in on what we've found out so far. If he's for it, tomorrow morning me and you will go bring them Diamond cattle back home." I kind of grinned at him when I said it.

He smiled back and said, "I'd be happy to help them find their way home."

I found my bunk and was asleep in no time. It was getting late in the afternoon when Josh shook me.

"Wake up and wash your face boy. We've been invited up to the house for supper. The boss and Sam want to hear about all that went on in town. You forgot to tell me about your meeting with the two gunslingers that killed Mills and shot up Jed."

"It wasn't much to tell. I met with them. We talked a mite. They decided to call their gunslinging days over and leave town."

Josh laughed and said, "Yep, that's just how Jed told it."

I got up, washed and changed shirts, and the two of us walked up to the house. Sam met us at the door and she was as pretty as ever. She had on a shirt and britches instead of a dress this time. I had about decided she would be pretty in about anything.

"Come in Reed. I wanted to thank you for getting Jed back to the ranch."

"My pleasure, Mam'."

"Don't Mam' me. You just call me Sam. All right?"

"Yes Mam'. I mean, all right Sam."

She laughed and said, "Come on back to the table. I've got Dad sitting in a chair back there and he said he was hungry enough to eat a side of beef. He's feeling a lot stronger."

We followed her and found Mr. Forbes with a smile on his face and a hand stretched out to shake ours.

"It's good to have you both back. I want to thank you Haddok for what you've done."

"I haven't done anything," I responded.

"Oh yes you have, if what Jed told us is true. You've settled a score for our men and don't think there's not a man on this place that don't feel beholding to you."

We set down to eat and Josh and me filled him in on what we had learned. He listened to us and when we had finished, he said, "I'm not going to wait for somebody to come clean out this bunch of rattlesnakes. I've got about one more week before I can set a horse and as soon as I can, we are going to the Bar J and do our own cleaning. You two get my cattle back here before they get them branded and I'll be obliged to you."

We told him we'd get it done and continued to talk and eat. After we had finished and said our goodnights, Sam followed us out on the porch and asked if she could talk to me alone for a minute. Josh tipped his hat and walked on toward the bunkhouse.

Sam looked me in the eye with those beautiful eyes of hers and said, "You are some strange man. There's a part of you that would make a woman proud to stand beside you, fight beside you, or if I might be so bold, sleep beside you. But then there's a side to you that scares me to death. Did you really cut those two men's fingers off?"

My face was red from what she had just said and I found myself searching for the right words.

"Yes, Sam. I cut their fingers off. It didn't bother me a bit. Those two men are killers and they never showed mercy to any man, woman, or kid that they set their sights on. They are lucky I didn't cut their throats. But there's one thing you need to understand. There will never be a reason for you to be scared of me, or of anyone else as long as I'm around." I looked her square in the eye and sort

71

of winked with a smile when I spoke. "Now, goodnight Mam'." I turned and walked away.

It would take me a long time to go to sleep tonight.

Come daylight me and Josh were ready to push off and bring the Diamond cattle back from the Bar J. We ate a quick breakfast of coffee and biscuits and said our farewells up at the house. We headed out to the northwest through some low hills and came to the place where Josh had picked up their trail. It was easy to follow and about an hour later we came up on what was left of the branded critters that the rustlers had shot. I made out nine of them. The route the rustlers took kept them to the low ground. A man would have been lucky to have seen them moving the cows.

We had been riding about three hours when we topped out on a hill and saw below us a sprawling valley with a small mouth to a canyon leading off to the north.

Pointing to the canyon, Josh said, "The cows are being held up there. We can hang back on the east side of this ridge and cross over a little after that treeline begins up yonder." He pointed up the ridge to our right. "We'll come down right on top of their men if they haven't moved."

I nodded my approval and we dropped back about half way down the hill and rode around. When we headed back up toward the trees I could hear the cattle bawling. I could also smell smoke and figured they were starting to brand the cattle, if not already at it.

We eased through the trees and stopped just over the crest of the hill, stepped out of our saddles with rifles in hand, and silently moved down toward the fire we had located by its smoke.

A little later we could hear the men talking and they were completely unaware of our presence. Alert for anything, we moved to where we could see them. Sure enough, there were three men setting by the fire drinking coffee. They had their backs to us. We eased out and walked to about twenty paces from them. I broke the silence.

"If you men hold them coffee cups real still and do just what I say, you may live to see the sun go down today."

You would have thought they had been struck by lightning. To a man they flinched, and then held real still.

"What do you want?" the older man of the three asked.

"My name is Haddok and I ride for the Diamond. You men are holding Diamond stock and we came to take them home."

The same feller said, "We didn't know they was stole, although we've been trying to figure out why they are all young stuff with no brands. Sledge just sent us up here to watch them for a few days and to get them branded."

"Well, you're in a good spot to get strung from a tree." We moved around in front of them and they looked nothing like gunfighters. "I'll tell you what I want you to do. Ease your guns out and lay them on the ground. Leave your rifles right where they lay. Saddle up and start them cows back toward the Diamond. We are going to be watching you from up on the hill. If you try to run or do anything funny, we'll kill you. You won't have time to make it to cover. Believe me, I haven't missed a shot this easy since I was ten years old."

"You won't have to watch us mister," the old man said. "We ain't rustlers and we want no part in it. We hired on to work cows and that's all we're getting paid for."

I answered, "I understand a man needs a job. But you men have hired on with a rotten bunch. If I was you, I'd find me a new place to work. You can tell Sledge I came and got the cows and when we get them back home, I'm gonna come and get him."

"I'll do it," he said as they placed their guns carefully to the ground and saddled up.

Josh said, "Ya'll push them back over onto Diamond land and then ride off. You won't see us, but we'll be watching you."

They went to work heading the cows out of the canyon and we stood up the hill watching. We made it back to our horses and held in the trees as they pointed the cattle toward the Diamond.

Josh asked as we rode, "Did you believe those men?"

"Yep!"

"Me to!"

About an hour later we watched from the high ground as the cowboys pulled up and sat looking at the cattle as they continued to move toward home. They then turned and rode slowly back toward their camp.

We rode down and kept the cattle moving. It had been easier than I thought and I felt good about it. I was riding light in the saddle and hardly felt it when my horse stepped down in a small hole. Those few inches probably saved my life. Just as he stepped down I heard a volley of rifle shots and felt a wicked blow to my head. Knocked out of the saddle, I blacked out on the way to the ground.

After I don't know how long, I came to with my head busting and blood running down my neck. Without moving, I tried to focus my eyes. From the way my head was laying, I could make out Josh about twenty paces from me. He was laying dead still. I could see the blood on his shirt and the ground around him was soaked with blood. I knew he was hurt bad, if not dead. His horse was standing about thirty feet beyond him with its head down. I was looking at Josh through low brush and remembered I had been riding through some when the shots rang out. It might be possible that where I lay the shooters could not see me. I took the risk and turned my head. There was brush all around me. I felt my head and I had a deep graze along the back side of it. It didn't seem to be bad, but it sure hurt. I had lost some blood, but not as much as Josh. I tried to think. I had to get Josh some help if he was still alive. I was pretty certain the shooters wouldn't leave until they were sure of their kill. I looked back at Josh and it was then I noticed his pistol was out of his holster and that his right hand was under his body. I saw his eyes blink as he looked in my direction.

I spoke softly. "Hold on and be still. They will come down here before long."

I crawled away from the spot where I fell and moved myself through the brush being careful not to shake any of the limbs. When I was about twenty-five paces downhill I rolled over where I could see Josh's horse. Then I waited.

Josh had heard the first rifle shot a split second before the next two. In that brief moment he had thrown himself off his horse away from the sound of the rifle fire. He had felt the slug rip into his side above his belt and along his back. On the way down he had pulled his pistol while the shooter's view had been blocked by his horse. He landed with his pistol in his hand tucked up under his chest. He was laying face down with his head turned toward the direction the shots came from. He had not seen Reed fall and expected him dead until he heard him speak.

So, for now, the two of them lay waiting on the men who shot them. Josh had disciplined himself to remain motionless for what seemed like an eternity. Reed had positioned himself to offer a surprise for the shooters.

The wait was on.

The three ambushers had been up at first light with their eyes on the ranch. Slay had picked out his man as Josh and Reed rode away from the ranch. The black horse with the white stockings gave him away. The two were riding around to the east of their position. They saddled up and rode north and then east to cut their trail. When they did, they followed the Diamond men carefully, hoping to not give away their presence. They found where the two had stopped near the carcasses of the dead cattle and noticed that they continued to follow the cattle tracks.

"They're tailing that bunch we rustled the other day," Mead declared.

Bolton asked, "What do you suppose they are up to?"

Slay pondered for a minute and said, "I'd bet they've gone after the cattle. That'll make it easy. We'll just find us a spot up ahead where we can get a good shot and then wait. They will be easy pickins while driving them cows."

The three rode on and moved to the high ground while watching the trail of the cattle. They found their spot about thirty minutes later. It was an outcropping of rocks that allowed them a full view of the trail. If they came back the same way, they would have them right where they wanted them. They hid their horses, lit them a smoke, and settled down to wait. Waiting was always a part of a backshooter's work. With one of them watching the trail, they discussed their plan.

Slay spoke first. "Haddok is mine. We'll all get paid, but I want him. You two take the other man. When they come, we'll all get ready and you let me shoot first. The two of you can use my shot as your signal and then take your man."

Bolton said, "It sounds easy enough for me."

Mead agreed.

The wait drug on and the sun got hot where they were waiting. Sweat ran down their faces and their clothes began to show wetness. They were fairly miserable and were about to give it up for another try somewhere else. Bolton had just said they must have misfigured when they heard the cattle. All three jumped into their firing positions and were settled when the first of the cattle came into view.

Slay whispered, "Let them come on. We want them as close as we can get them."

The cattle kept coming and finally the two riders came into view. They were riding careful, looking all around. But they were boxed in and right where the ambushers wanted them. Haddok was nearer to them and Slay put his sights on him. Looking down the barrel, he followed him as he rode closer. A thrill rose up in his throat.

All three ambushers indicated they were ready. Slay put his front sight right on Haddok's head and breathed in calmly. This was a sure thing. He took up the slack of his trigger and began to squeeze. The rifle bucked against his shoulder with a roar and his man crumpled to the ground. Right on the heels of his shot came the shots of Bolton and Mead as they emptied the saddle of the other man. The cattle raced on ahead in a jump as the deafening sound of the rifle fire echoed down the draw. Then it was quiet.

All was still.

Slay could make out the man with Haddok easily and blood was already spreading across his shirt. He could not see Haddok because he had fallen into the belly high brush he was riding through. It didn't make any difference though. He knew Haddok was laying in there with half his head blowed off.

They watched and listened. They saw nothing nor heard anything. Haddok's horse had run off about fifty feet and stopped. He was just standing there. The other man's horse had shied when the shots were fired but he stopped a short distance from the man and was looking around.

Slay took out his glass and studied the area carefully. They waited. There was no movement or sound. But they still waited. Finally Bolton spoke.

"What we waiting for. Let's ride. They both are dead."

Slay said, "We are going to go down and make sure. Let's wait a little longer."

After about thirty minutes, they went to their horses, mounted up, and rode down. They all three were relaxed and knew the extra money was already in their pockets.

They spread out onto the flat ground and headed in the direction of their targets. The horse belonging to the man who rode with Haddok raised his head and snorted when they leveled out into the draw. Rifles ready, they rode on up.

Bolton said, "I'm gonna put another slug in this one." He gestured toward Josh. As the words cleared his throat and he started to bring his rifle around toward Josh, a shot rang out. The slug caught Bolton in the throat and he was dead when he left the saddle. Slay turned toward the sound of the shot only to hear another. This one came from behind them and from Josh's pistol. The slug caught Mead in the back of the head and he too fell face forward into the dust.

Slay looked both ways and knew he was a dead man if he did anything. To his left was the man riding with Haddok and, surprisingly, he didn't look dead at all. His pistol was pointing square at Slay's chest. To his right was the man he figured to be Haddok. He was standing in that waist high brush looking right down his pistol sights at him.

Slay spoke, "Hold it now. This wasn't my idea. I just rode along with these two. I didn't even like them and I don't care that they're dead."

Haddok said, "Drop your rifle and step down. Keep your hands where I can see them."

Slay did just as he was told. When he got both feet on the ground he looked around to find that Haddok had stepped out of the brush and was facing him with his pistol back in the holster.

Haddok said calmly, "I'm gonna kill you. You can draw or just stand there. I don't care."

Slay pled, "Now listen. I ain't no gunfighter. I don't want no part of this. You've got the wrong—" As he was talking he was looking for an edge and his hand dropped quickly to his pistol and he started to draw. He could not believe his eyes. The man hardly moved, and yet his pistol was in his hand, jumping in quick barks as three slugs tore into his chest. He continued his draw but his hand felt empty and Haddok was standing in bright light that suddenly grew dim. He never knew it when he hit the ground, face first.

Haddok looked over at Josh to find him standing. He was weak, but standing.

Josh said, "Get my horse and help me on him. I've lost a lot of blood and I don't know how long I can hold out."

"Sure thing! I'll get you back to the ranch." He checked Josh's wound. It was deep, but the bullet had hit him at an angle across the muscle of his back. There was an entrance wound and an exit wound. The bleeding had about stopped. He gave Josh some water from his canteen. He then plugged the wounds with some small pieces of cloth he cut from Josh's shirt. He cut some strips and tied the plugs tight around his body. He laid Josh down and said, "You hold on here for a minute. I've got something to do."

He cut some rope and threw all three dead men across their saddles. He tied their feet and hands together beneath the horses bellies. In one last act, he pulled his knife and in successive strokes he sliced off the trigger fingers of the dead men. He then pulled his pistol and fired twice as the horses bolted and ran out of there carrying the remains of the ambushers. He then walked over and lifted Josh to help him into the saddle.

Josh said, "Man, you know how to leave a trail."

"I want their boss to know I'm still alive and I want the rest of his hired guns to know what they are up against. It won't hurt to play with their minds a little bit."

"Well, that ought to do it. So now you've finally killed a man."

"Yep! That first one left me no choice. He was about to shoot you again."

"What about the last one?"

"I had to kill him before you did." Haddok grinned at him. "Now, hush talking and let's get you to the ranch."

Haddok got him in the saddle, stepped into his own, and they rode out at a walk headed for the Diamond.

Beecham was furious when the three cowhands rode in at the Bar J. They told how Haddok and another man had come and driven the cattle they were keeping back to the Diamond ranch. The older cowhand didn't tell the whole story. He and the other two had decided they ought to leave out the part about them helping.

"They got the drop on us and there wasn't one thing we could do."

Beecham and Sledge were listening to their story.

Beecham asked, "You say it was Haddok?"

"Yes sir! He told us his name. He said that the cattle had been stole from the Diamond and that they were going to take them back. I told him we didn't know anything about stolen cattle. I told him that Sledge had sent us out to keep them and brand them. That was when he told us that as soon as he got them cattle home he was going to come after you Sledge."

The old man's words caused a chill to go down Sledge's back and he tried to conceal their effect. Only a man watching him close would have picked up the nervous way he swallowed.

"Well, let him come," Sledge said. "But he may not make it. I've got some good men looking for him right now."

Beecham looked over at Sledge and said, "I'm paying you and your men good money. I'm tired of this man Haddok. I want him taken care of. Do you understand me?"

"Sure boss. You don't have nothing to worry about."

Beecham turned and went into the house. Sledge sent the three men over to help some other cowhands and he made his way to the bunkhouse that the gunslingers used when they were on the ranch. He walked in and asked the four men playing cards if they had heard anything from Slay. Getting a no for an answer, he flopped down on a bunk and began to think through this man Haddok. He wouldn't know him if he saw him. Up to now he had cost him five men and a lot of trouble. If Slay, Mead, and Bolton couldn't handle the job, he might just have to do it himself. While he was thinking, he drifted off to sleep. He woke up with a start from the yelling that was going on outside.

Sledge jumped up and raced through the door with his gun

pulled. He found his men holding three horses with the bodies of Bolton, Mead, and Slay tied across the saddles. The gunslingers and cowhands were gathered around. Beecham was walking fast across the yard.

They untied the men and laid them on the ground.

"Bolton got it clean through the neck," one of them said.

"Slay has three holes in his chest that you could cover with a silver dollar," another exclaimed.

"Mead caught it right in the back of the head," a third man declared.

"Look at their hands," someone shouted. "All their trigger fingers have been cut off—as clean as a whistle."

Sledge didn't answer. He quickly ordered the men to bury them. He walked back to the bunkhouse. This wasn't working out like he had planned. Running over ranchers was one thing. Haddok was something else. The total was now eight men he had lost to him. The number would rise to twelve before tomorrow because four more of his gunhands would ride off during the night without as much as saying goodbye. Being dead was one thing. Being dead without a trigger finger was something else.

As the burial detail started their work, to the southeast another group of men, led by Gus Trapp and made up of six Diamond riders, were beginning their search for Reed Haddok and Josh Spencer. A cowhand had reported that a herd of young unbranded cattle had come pounding onto Diamond rangeland. The Diamond men knew that Haddok and Spencer had gone to retrieve the cattle. Mr. Forbes had sent Gus to search for them. They followed the path of the cattle and about an hour out from the ranch they came up on the wounded men riding slowly toward the ranch. They led them on to the ranch, sending a rider to tell the folks at the ranch to get the water hot. Wounded men were on their way.

When Sam saw their condition, she ordered them both brought into the house. She dispatched a rider to Prescott to fetch Doc Summers. Her makeshift doctor's ward now had grown to four patients.

When Haddok woke up, it was to the feel of soft hands carefully washing the back of his head with warm water. He remembered riding into the ranch yard and being helped down from his horse. He barely remembered being lowered to a bed. Sam was sitting on the side of his bed with a pan of soapy water and a cloth in her hand.

"Be still. This is a nasty crease in the back of your head."

"How is Josh?"

"He's mighty weak and running a fever. I've got the bleeding stopped and the wounds are cleaned out the best I could do. We've sent a man to Prescott to get the doctor. It will be late in the day before he can get here."

"Where is he?"

"He's in the room next door. This is my room you are in."

She continued to work on his wound and Haddok began to relax under her tender touch.

Sam inquired, "What happened out there?"

"We found the cattle and started them back. On the way we were ambushed. They must have been watching the ranch and tailed us. It was a perfect set-up and if they had any luck at all, me and Josh would be dead."

"Did you see them or could you recognize them if you saw them again?"

"I won't see them again. The last time I did see them they were cold dead and hung over their horses. The horses were running full out toward the Bar J."

"You killed them?"

"Yep! They picked the wrong job."

"Well, I'm proud. I've got kind of used to you around here and I sure don't want you getting killed." She smiled that snow-melting smile when she said it.

Haddok noticed his shirt was off and he embarrassingly felt to see if his britches were gone too. He was relieved to find them still on. He lay still as she doctored him with some kind of ointment. She then ordered him to get some rest. She left the room and Haddok soon drifted off the sleep.

After a while he woke up to the smell of coffee and soup. Sam made him sit up in the bed and she packed some pillows behind him. She set a tray in his lap. The coffee and soup were steaming hot. On the side of the tray were three pieces of bread covered up with lots of butter.

"Eat up," she said as she walked out of the room. Haddok watched her leave and thought to himself that with this kind of treatment, he might never get well.

Sam was in and out of the room often during the day and she

always reported on Josh before Haddok could ask about him. Her last report was that his fever was high. She said she was sticking pretty close to him. Late in the afternoon Haddok heard the commotion as the doctor entered the house and went straight to Josh's room. It was a long while before he entered Haddok's room and set down on the side of the bed to look at his wound.

"It's not too bad, but you are a lucky man. Matter of fact, both of you are lucky. Your friend has a mean bullet hole through the muscle in his lower back. I don't think it damaged anything else. He's going to be laid up for a while. The good news is that he will be all right in time. His fever is coming down some. He's going to be real sore for a spell. As for you, a couple inches difference and you would be dead."

After the doctor left, Haddok swung his legs off the bed and stood up for a minute. He was groggy, but it felt good to stand. While he was standing, Sam came through the door.

"I've spent all night and day making sure you two live. I'm not about to let you get up and leave now. Get back in that bed."

"Yes mam'," Haddok said with a winsome grin as he eased himself down.

But after supper and into the early night, he would slip out of the bed and stand or walk around the room. He was feeling better all the while and he wanted out of there as quick as possible. He had some work to do.

He slept well through the night and was up at the smell of coffee the next morning. He found his shirt, washed and folded, on the foot of his bed. His pistol and hat were on a chair. Dressing and washing his face from the pan of water in the room, he then made his way to the coffee. Mr. Forbes, Gus, and Sam were seated at the table when he walked in.

"Good morning," Haddok said.

They looked up and greeted him with smiles and handshakes.

Gus spoke, "You look a lot better."

"A man would have to with the kind of nursing I've been getting. How's Josh?"

Sam responded. Her cheeks were blushed from Haddok's remark. "He's better. He slept most of the night and his fever is gone."

"Good. I thought for a while out there he was dead. He's one tough man. He still had a lot of fight in him when most folks would have given up."

They talked and Sam served them breakfast.

Forbes told them of his plans. "I need a few more days before I'm back to full strength. As soon as I'm ready, we are going to the Bar J and settle the score."

"That won't be necessary," Haddok said. "They won't be there."

"Why not?", Forbes asked.

"Because I'm going to go over there and ask them to leave."

Forbes laughed and said, "Ask them to leave? Do you think they will leave because you ask them to?"

"They have been running roughshod over you folks for almost a year now. They killed one of your men and shot up another. They shot you from ambush. They've rustled your cattle and salted your ponds. They nearly killed my best friend and tried to kill me. Yes sir! When I get through asking them, I think they will want to leave."

"I can't let you go by yourself. They will kill you."

"I've been handling things by myself for a long time."

Sam injected, "Reed, I don't want you to go. We need you here."

"Oh, don't get me wrong. I don't want to go. This is one of those times when they have left me no choice. But don't you worry about me. I'd rather fight all the men on the Bar J at one time than to fight my sister, and she's the one who taught me to fight." Haddok said that to try to lighten their spirits a mite. It didn't help though as they continued to persuade him to wait.

Haddok finally left the room and went to Josh's and set down on the chair beside his bed. They were proud to see each other. They talked a while and Haddok told him of his plans to go to the Bar J.

"Be careful, Bud. That's a rough bunch of killers they've got over there. Don't show no mercy. If you do, you'll be dead."

"Don't you worry. Their mercy ran out when they ambushed you and me. From here on they all are on that list that gave me no choice."

Haddok spent the rest of the day cleaning his weapons. He ate plenty of food to get his strength back. Every now and then he would catch a glimpse of Sam. After supper, he sat down on the porch and was watching the sun set. Sam came out and sat down beside him.

"Reed, tell me about your folks. You mentioned a sister earlier today. I would like to know about your family."

Haddok started in talking and never felt it come so easy. Sam listened as if it was important. He told her about the ranch back in

Texas and how they had worked hard to make it. He told her about his mother and how good she was. He told how it hurt when she died. He spoke of his father and how he liked to wander. He also told how his father took time to teach him and his sister the things that really mattered. He told about Tess and how proud he was of her. He mentioned how close they were even though she tried to boss him around when he was young. He revealed his dream to see the red hills and how he would like to have a ranch of his own.

Sam listened to him talk and said she would love to meet his sister. Before they knew it they had talked well into the night. Haddok couldn't believe he had done most of the talking.

Finally, Sam touched Haddok's hand and said, "Reed, I can't keep you from going to the Bar J. I'm not sure I even want to. If I was a man, I would have already gone myself. I just want you to know that it is very important to me that you come back."

With that said, she leaned over and kissed Haddok a peck on the cheek. She then hurried into the house. Haddok sat there feeling the heat of his face and his nose full of her sweet smell. At that minute he knew that he was coming back if he had to crawl through hell to get there.

He went inside to get some sleep. Tomorrow was going to be a busy day. When he fell into bed and thought back over the last few minutes, he felt something he had never experienced before. There was a reason for Reed Haddok to live.

The chill of the early morning felt good. I had left out about three hours before sunrise without saying anything to anybody. My horse was rested and full of spunk. He was moving at a steady clip as I rode off of Diamond land and onto some open range that lay between us and the Bar J. The moon was bright and I wanted to get as close to their ranch as I could before daylight. I didn't know how many gunhands they had and I wanted to know all I could before they knew I was around.

It was getting close to first light when I topped out on a rise and saw what seemed to be a bunch of buildings off to my left. I figured it to be the Bar J ranch house and out buildings. There were already lights on in the house and what was probably the bunkhouse. The ranch itself set back against a small mountain. A large valley sprawled out before it. Their view and field of fire was perfect if trouble came their way. No large group could get at them from the rear.

However, one man might be able to come down off that mountain unnoticed. I began to work my way around to that mountain. I was half way up it and under the cover of trees when the sun finally popped up over the high ground from where I first saw the ranch. I made my way higher until I was directly behind the ranch. I stepped out of the saddle and tied my horse. With my rifle in hand I began to slip down toward the ranch. I pulled up when I got to a spot where I could see the layout of the buildings clearly. I was careful to move slowly because the early sunlight was square on me and I might be spotted if they had someone watching their backdoor. I settled down in some brush.

I watched as cowhands busied themselves getting their day started. There were also three gunslingers stationed around the house and I figured them to be the lookouts. All three wore tied-down guns and carried rifles. It was obvious they were spooked. I had hoped that getting a look at their three drygulchling buddies tied to their horses might accomplish just that.

After it got shady where I was setting, I eased back up to my horse and got my canteen and some jerked beef from my saddle bags. I made my way back down and settled in for a while.

As I waited, I got to thinking about my situation. When I left Texas I never dreamed of being in this kind of conflict. There was no denying the fact that Samantha had struck a chord in my heart. Her father was a good man and was trying to make an honest living. The men who worked for him were loyal.

Beecham was the kind of man who could eat dinner in the presence of someone he had just killed. I asked myself why I was here on the side of this mountain. Was it for Sam or her father? Was it because Beecham had tried to have me killed? Was it for fame? I came to the conclusion that it was because somebody needed to be here and I was the man. Live or die, there comes a time when a man has to stand for what is right. Some are better prepared to make that stand than others. Thanks to my paw and Josh, I figured I was as prepared as a man could be.

As I set there thinking, I noticed a man walk up to one of the lookouts and they stood there talking a spell. The man was the gunman I had seen in the cafe with Beecham the first and only time

I had seen him. I would have bet my winter wages he was the man they called Sledge.

I watched him walk back around the house. I noticed that he wore black britches and a black hat with a tan vest over a light colored shirt. I wanted Sledge. I wanted him as bad as I wanted Beecham. I fought the urge to walk right down there shooting. With as many men as they had, I needed an edge. I needed to get Sledge away from the house. I practiced my best edge for the moment. Surprise is always on your side. I waited.

About the middle of the afternoon I got lucky. I saw Sledge and one of the lookouts saddle up and ride off to my right. I figured the route they traveled was the road from the ranch to Prescott. I hurried back up the mountain to my horse. I hit the saddle and rode right back over the mountain and down toward where I figured their route would take them. Sure enough, I saw them ride down into a wash that would bring them my way. I rode on ahead of them and pulled up in a scope of trees that guarded the rim of the wash they were riding in. Slipping out of the saddle, I left my rifle on the horse and scooted down the steep side of the wash. I came to a rest in some bushes that flanked the wall of the wash. I heard them coming and hardly had time to think before they rode right by me. I stepped out behind them and yelled.

"Hold it right there."

They reined up and started to look around.

"Keep your eyes straight ahead or I'll blow you both out of the saddle. Keep your hands where I can see them and step down."

They did just what I told them and when they stepped down out of the saddle they stood facing away from me with their hands away from their guns. I had the drop on them and they were not about to try anything.

"Now turn around and face me."

They turned to see me for the first time and there was a mixture of fear and suspense in their eyes.

"Walk back this way and get out of the way of your horses."

They walked a few paces toward me and off to the side of their horses.

"My name is Haddok. I've come to kill you Sledge."

Sledge responded, "Well, now. Are you going to shoot me with my hands in the air or are you going to give me a chance to draw?"

"I ought to have shot you in the back. That seems to be the way you and your men fight. You can be sure I am going to have you looking right at me when I kill you. However, I'm not going to take the time to bury you. I'll let the buzzards take care of you. But, if it means anything to you, I will bury your trigger finger before I leave."

Sledge looked a little pale when I said that and his buddy looked sick. Sledge was mean all right and I had no doubt he was good with his pistol. Thinking back on what Josh had taught me, my first bullet would be for Sledge and my second for his partner. In a swift move I dropped my pistol into the holster. There we stood, facing each other, with death dancing in the fifteen paces between us. I felt as calm as I had ever felt in my life. I really didn't understand why. I spoke.

"Any time you're ready."

I looked Sledge square in the eye. My outer vision was locked on his partner. All I waited on was the flexing of a muscle from either one of them. I saw it. I drew and fired twice. The first bullet caught Sledge in the mouth and he was dead before you could blink your eye. The second went through the gunhand of his partner as he drew. Neither of them cleared leather. Sledge's buddy was down on the ground holding his bleeding hand and if it had not been so serious, it would have been funny. He blurted these words.

"Please man. Don't cut my finger off."

"If you do exactly as I say, you may keep your finger and your life. If I had wanted you dead, you'd be dead. I hit you right where I meant to hit you."

I pulled his pistol from his belt and gathered Sledge's pistol and threw them both into the bushes.

"How many gunslingers are still at the Bar J?"

"There's not but six of us still there. I knew I should have left with the others."

"Now listen to me. I'm going to give you a chance to live. I want you to get on your horse and ride back to the ranch. Tell the gunslingers that I am coming and that I am going to kill whoever is still there. Do you understand me?"

"Yes sir! I'll go right now and tell them."

"No you won't. You'll stay right here for about an hour and then you will go. I'll be watching you and you are dead if you don't do what I say."

"Man, I might bleed to death in an hour."

"You don't deserve to live. Maybe I'll just go ahead and kill you right now."

"No! No! I'll wait," he exclaimed.

I climbed up the side of the wash. I kept my eye on the wounded man until I got to my horse and swung into the saddle. I rode out of there on the run and retraced my route back to the spot on the side of the mountain overlooking the ranch. I was watching when the man I had shot rode in at the ranch. He had cheated me a little on the hour I had told him to wait. However, I had enough time to get settled back in my place.

The wounded man, known as Taggart to his friends, pulled up at the bunkhouse and found himself surrounded by the remaining gunslingers and a group of cowhands. His hand had been bleeding a lot and he had it wrapped in what looked like Sledge's shirt. He blurted out in broken speech, "Haddok killed Sledge and winged me before either one of us could clear leather in a fair draw—fastest I've ever seen—I'm leaving now—he's coming—said he would kill all of you—I'm leaving—I'm not going to be here when he comes."

The gunslingers stood speechless. The man who brought them here was dead. They didn't like the way this thing was shaping up. They all went to their horses and saddled up. They rode out without saying a word to anyone.

Haddok watched all this from the high ground behind the ranch. This was his chance. It was a good bet that Beecham was down there without his protection. Haddok knew the man was tough. It was time to find out how tough.

I waited only a few minutes and then left my position to sneak down the mountain. I slipped up behind the ranch house. As I moved alongside the rear of the house, I heard voices coming from around the corner. Pulling up, I listened and made out these words.

"I'm not getting into this. I signed on to work cattle."

Others echoed the man who spoke. I stepped around the corner and found myself facing five men circled up and talking. They were startled when they saw me and to a man they stepped back and held their hands clear of their pistols. The old man I had talked to when we retook the Diamond cattle was the one who spoke.

"Haddok, we're not in this. We haven't been a part of Beecham's gunslingers. We all needed a job and we've done nothing more than ranching."

"Then ride out."

"If you don't mind, we'd like to hang around and watch. My name is Wells and these fellers are Hardy, Couples, Franks, and Ames. We don't hold to Beecham's ways. He's mistreated the lot of us at one time or another."

"You can stay, but get back out of my way."

With that, I eased myself around and stepped up on the porch. Looking through a window, I spotted Beecham seated at a desk. His back was to me and the front door. It was likely he knew nothing of his guards leaving. Walking on cat's feet, I went to the door and turned the knob. It was not locked. Easing the door open, I stepped inside with my pistol in my hand.

Beecham must have sensed someone's presence and he turned around to look into my calm eyes. I was the man he wanted dead, but he had never met me. He was cool. I couldn't help but think that if I had met this man out on the street, under different circumstances, I would probably have said sir to him. He looked like a man people would respect.

However, I came here to strip him of all the respect he had ever had, whether earned or demanded. As cool and respectable as he looked, I was not fooled into thinking this would be easy. I knew that beneath this man's exterior was a ruthlessness that could easily take my life. Even though I startled him with my presence, he didn't give it away. He broke the silence.

"What can I do for you?"

"My name is Haddok and I've come to show you that you're more fit for life back east somewhere."

"So, you're Haddok. Pull up a chair and sit down. I've been wanting to talk to you."

"Nope! I didn't come to talk. You stand up, careful like, and keep your hands where I can see them. If you try anything, you are a dead man."

Beecham didn't like it. He thought, where is Sledge and his men? He would go along and do as Haddok said until he saw his chance and then he would kill this stupid man. He stood up and turned to face Haddok, his hands in full view.

"I know you carry a hidden gun. Pull it out carefully."

Beecham thought, how does he know that?

"Now you pull it out and toss it to the floor. Believe me, I hope you give me a reason to shoot you."

Beecham reached inside his coat and pulled a pistol from his belt. He dropped it gingerly to the floor.

"You've got one more. I want it too."

Beecham extracted a two shot derringer from his sleeve and dropped it as well.

"Now, kick them over here."

Beecham did as he was told. I picked them up, walked to the door, and threw them out in the yard. I never took my eyes off the man. I calculated him to be one mean hombre. I walked back in front of him and spoke.

"Now this is what we are going to do. You are going to give me all the notes you hold on the ranchers around here and I'm going to burn them. Then you are going to deed me this ranch. Don't look shocked. I'm prepared to pay for it."

Beecham was laughing.

"You're crazy. I'll do no such a thing. You don't have the kind of money that would buy this place."

"Sure I do," I said with a chuckle of my own. I reached into my left pocket and pulled out a small fold of bills. I had carried them since that day back on the Brazos when I sent those three men hightailing who bothered my sister. "There's seven dollars here. I've been saving this for a long time. You can write on the deed that you sold me this ranch for the price of seven dollars and other considerations."

"Never," Beecham declared.

"Oh sure you will. Before I'm through with you, you'll want to."

I looked at the man. He easily weighed two hundred and forty pounds. He was not fat. His round thick shoulders and his large hands spoke of strength. While I was sizing him up, I remembered why I was here in the first place. I quickly holstered my pistol. When my right hand came up from that action I continued in one motion and threw a wicked right that caught him high on the cheek and it split his face open. The punch caught him by surprise and he landed on the desk in a sitting position. When he came off the desk he was smiling through the blood running down to the corner of his mouth. I knew then I had a fight on my hands.

"I'm going to beat you to death," he said. "You may be good with your gun, but no man has ever whipped me in a bare hand fight."

"My sister could beat you Beecham. Well! Come on."

Beecham waded in low and sent a blow to my belly that took my wind momentarily. He then threw a uppercut that caught me square on the chin. It set me on my back in the floor. Beecham knew he had me. He obviously had been here many times before. He rushed in and kicked me in the ribs with a glancing blow. I had rolled away from his kick just in time. He then kicked at my head and missed. I had rolled to my right away from the kick. Catching him off balance, I pushed his leg in the direction of the kick and threw him to the floor. We both rose and faced each other. I could hear my paw's words, "Keep getting up til you see quit in his eyes." I thought, it may be a while before this man quits.

Standing toe to toe, we traded punches. He carried power in his and each one hurt like the devil. I feinted with my left and he took the fake. I followed it with a right that shook him to his roots. I then grabbed him and hip rolled him to the floor.

99

He sprang up like a cat and again we stood toe to toe. While trading punches, he caught me with a left that felt like a mule kick. I was on the floor again looking up at this grinning man. I got up quickly and we continued to circle and throw punches. We both were more calculated now. Blood was streaming down from cuts on both our faces. I was beginning to think I might have roped the wrong bronc.

He caught me with a straight right that sent me to the floor again. Getting up, I decided I was getting tired of his grin and hitting that floor. A calm resolve took over my body. He saw it in my eyes and he didn't like it. He probably had never seen it before. I had taken his best punch three times during the course of the fight only to get back up. I could see some doubt come over him.

I walked in with assurance. I ducked his right and from low down threw a powerful blow to his mid-section. I followed it with another, and then another to the same spot. He was bending over gasping for air when I brought my knee up and crushed his face. I then stomped his right foot. He cried out in pain while I sent another crushing right to his belly. For all purposes it was over. I owned him.

Blow after blow landed on his face and he offered no return. I saw it in his eyes. Quit had finally come. He began to beg and to try to cover his face. With one more belly shot and a knee to the face, he set flat on the seat of his britches. He was a beaten man.

I stood over him and asked, "Now do you want to burn those notes and sell me the ranch?" He tried to say no. I hit him again square on the chin and sent him sprawling. Then I said, "Okay then, you tell me when you get ready to sell." I drew back to hit him again and he held up his hands to stop me.

"I'm ready," he muttered.

I pulled him up and put the chair under him. Then I told him, "Dig those notes out."

He fumbled in his desk. I stood right over him. He pulled out a stack of papers and handed them to me. I looked them over and saw that they were indeed loan papers. I found a match and walked over to the fireplace. I set fire to them, dropping them as they burned. I then told him, "Write me out a bill of sale for the ranch, including the mineral rights. Authorize the deed to be transferred to Reed Haddok and Josh Spencer." He didn't want to, but he had no choice. I then added, "Be sure to say the buying price is seven dollars and other considerations."

When he had finished and signed it, I handed him the seven dollars and said, "These are the other considerations. You are going to leave this country and never come back. You are more fit for life back east. If I were you, I'd change my name. I'm going to ask every stranger I meet if he has ever heard of you. I'm going to read the newspapers. I'm going to listen to the saloon talk. If I ever get a hint of your whereabouts I'm coming to look you up and kill you. Do you understand me?" With that question I hit him again.

Totally beaten, confused, and frightened, he whimpered that he understood.

"One other thing. I know you've been getting gold or silver out of the mountains on this ranch. I'm having your bank accounts frozen, based upon the bill of sale you've signed. Don't try to get that money. Do you understand?" I hit him again.

He began to beg me not to hit him anymore. His eyes were now almost swollen shut, his nose crushed, and blood was seeping from numerous cuts on his face.

I pulled him to his feet and drew my knife. It was obvious that he had never known or felt such fear. I cut his coat off of him and then his shirt. Next came the belt and britches. His drawers were the last to fall. I then had him remove his boots and socks. Completely naked, he was a pitiful beaten sight. I walked him to the door and pushed him out into the yard. By now eleven cowhands stood watching the spectacle.

"Get a horse and put him on it. No saddle!"

One of the men ran to the corral and came back shortly with a horse. The men lifted him onto the horse and stepped back. His head hung in shame. I walked over close and said in a low voice. "I do hope to see you again sometime." With that, I slapped the horse on the flank and it bolted out of the yard with its rider trying to stay on.

I turned to the men who had watched the whole thing and said, "Me and Josh Spencer now own this ranch. Do you men need a job?"

The old man named Wells spoke, "If you will have me, I'd be mighty proud to work for you."

To a man they all indicated that they would like to stay on.

I responded, "The ranch will be the Rocking H. I'll expect you to ride for the brand and I won't ask you to do nothing I won't do. I'll pay you a fare wage and treat you like a man. I will want you to ride and work in pairs for the next month or so until I am sure none of Beecham's gunslingers decide to come back for my hide. I expect you to let me know if you see any of his men hanging around."

They agreed and I started back toward the house when I was

stopped by one of the cowhands. The man was big and had a full beard. The man said, "Haddok, my name is Ames. When I heard you was over at the Diamond, I started to leave this neck of the woods. I probably should have."

I noticed that the man was unsure of himself and he gave me the feeling that he was frightened.

Ames continued, "My problem is that I've met a Mexican woman. She has two kids. Her husband was killed a while back while breaking horses. She's a fine woman and I want to marry her."

"What's that got to do with me?"

"Well, I'm trying to get to that. I threw in with the wrong crowd a few years back and found myself going against my raising. A feller helped me realize how far I'd wandered from my mama's teaching. I've walked a pretty straight path since then."

Still puzzled, I said, "So?"

"I know just how Beecham felt leaving out of here buck naked." Saying that, he turned his face a might and I could see a scar line beneath his beard running from his ear across to the corner of his mouth.

I looked Ames in the eye for a long moment. I then smiled and asked, "Can this Mexican woman cook?"

"Best I ever seen," he replied.

"Well then, go marry her and bring her and them kids back here as soon as you can. They can stay in the ranch house for the time being. By the way, I'm mighty proud you found your way back to your mama's teaching." I grinned and walked away.

As I went into the house, still smiling at this strange turn of events, I thought, I'll tell Ames one day I bought this ranch with his pistol and money that was part his.

Two weeks had passed since Haddok had his showdown with Beecham. In that time he had transferred the deed to the ranch into his and Josh's names under the Rocking H brand. He had also spoken to the sheriff and told him of the sudden departure of Beecham. Like always, he didn't go into the details. The sheriff had learned them from the cowhands who were present when Haddok had run Beecham off. It brought a big smile to his face.

Haddok also went to the bank and froze all Beecham's accounts. He told the banker that it all would be settled in accordance with the law and he intended for Beecham's money to go to the people he had cheated and the families of the people he had killed. He told the banker that if one penny of Beecham's money left the bank without him knowing about it, he would personally run him out of town. The banker understood.

During the two weeks he had learned that the mining operation on the ranch was for gold. It was in the early stages and the actual mining had not been up and running long. He put a hold on the mining operation and let the men go who were working there.

The word got out plenty fast that Haddok had burned the notes Beecham held on the people around Prescott. He became a popular man overnight. He gave the ranchers he could contact permission to go back to their ranches. He told them he would sign the necessary papers as soon as possible. He invited them to come to the ranch and sort out any of their cattle they could identify. Haddok was a big man in their circles.

During the time that had passed, Mr. Forbes had got up and about the ranch. Josh was sitting up some, but was still mighty sore. The wound to the muscles in his back would take a long time to heal. Haddok had sent a rider soon after the showdown to tell Josh that the two of them were now owners of the former Bar J. It was now the Rocking H ranch. The messenger told Josh that his boss had said, "Hurry and get well. You are not helping much setting around and letting Sam cook for you and nurse maid you." Josh had laughed when he got that message. He thought, me and Reed with our own ranch. What about that? The cowhand then filled in all the details of what Haddok had done. Josh, Mr. Forbes, and Sam had listened intently, asking questions from time to time, and hearing it all in disbelief.

Sam finally asked, "How is Reed? Was he hurt?"

The fellow told them that he looked fairly beat-up after running Beecham off, but was quick to add that Beecham looked a sight worse. The cowhand ended by saying, "Our boss is some kind of man."

Sam replied, almost to herself, "He certainly is that."

It was a quiet morning in Prescott when the tall man rode in. His dark hat was pulled down and he wore a slicker that was open down the front. His gun was tied down. His eyes took in the town as he rode up in front of the bank and stepped out of the saddle. He continued to look up and down the street as he tied his horse to the rail. He thought to himself, this don't look like a town that needs to be tamed.

He walked into the bank and asked to speak to the banker. His walk and voice carried a certain confidence. When the banker came out of his office, the stranger spoke in a low voice. "You should have an envelope here for me. It will have Doc printed on the outside."

The banker looked him over nervously and said, "Yes sir. I have it. I'll be right back."

The banker went to his desk and came back with the envelope. He extended it to the stranger. Doc took it without saying a word and turned and walked out of the bank. Standing beside his horse, he opened the envelope and counted one thousand dollars in bills. He folded it and placed it in his pocket. This was his first payment that he required for every job. When he finished, there was to be another thousand. Regardless of how big or small the job, he always got the first payment before he started to work. There had been a few times when his presence was all that was needed to clean up a town. The rough lot had left without him having to fire a shot. In those cases he never claimed the finish money.

Unhitching his horse, he walked across to the sheriff's office, tied him again, and walked in. The sheriff stood to meet him and the stranger spoke.

"I'm Doc. I've been sent for to settle some folks down here in Prescott. I always work within the law. I'd like to have your support. I won't need your help."

The sheriff smiled and responded, "It's good to meet you. I've heard a lot about you and it has all been good. A few weeks back I would have hugged you when you walked in. But you are a little late. We had a young man by the name of Haddok who hired on out at the Diamond last winter. The Diamond was one of the main targets of a bunch of gunslingers. A man by the name of Beecham had hired them. They had been running roughshod over everybody and swindling people out of their land. They set their sights on the Diamond and ran into Haddok. Well, let me tell you, Haddok is a curly wolf. He got his dander up and he has fairly cleaned this place up so it's more like a church social than anything else."

Doc pulled up a chair with an astonished smile on his face and said, "Tell me the whole story."

The sheriff talked and Doc listened for well over an hour. When Doc had heard it all, he stood and shook the sheriff's hand and thanked him. He asked directions to the Diamond and left, telling the sheriff he was headed back to Texas.

It was well after dark when Doc rode up behind the barn at the Diamond. He hitched his horse and walked silently in the shadows until he was up beside the house. Josh was sitting in a chair at the end of the porch. He was startled when he heard the familiar voice.

"How you feeling Spence?"

Without turning, Josh laughed and said, "Pretty good for a shot-up old man. I heard they had sent for you."

"Well, it looks like I'm a little late. How's my boy?"

"He's fine. You don't need to worry about him."

"Where is he?"

"He's over at our new ranch. Mr. Forbes and Samantha rode over there today to check on him. They were going to stay the night. They had not seen him since the big showdown two weeks ago."

"Does he know about me?"

"Nope! I never told him. I figured I'd let you do that when you wanted to."

"Thanks! I'll always owe you Spence. You've been a good friend. I will always appreciate you for catching up with him when he left the Brazos and for watching after him."

"He don't need much watching. You've got yourself one fine boy."

"Did he do all I've heard he did?"

"You probably haven't heard it all. I'll tell you the rest some day."

"Don't tell him about me or my being here. I'm going to head back toward Texas. I left Tess with a sight of work to do. I think I'm going to stick close to ranching from now on. I might be getting a little old for this kind of work."

Josh chuckled and said, "You're still a hand full and you know it. But let me tell you, the boy is good. Believe it or not, he's faster with his six-gun than you were in your prime."

Josh couldn't see the pride in Doc's eyes as he said it, but he heard it in his voice.

108

"He's that good, huh?"

"Yep. But he's like you. He'll walk all the way around the house to keep from killing. He's one of the few that can handle being good."

"I hear he's pretty good with his grandpaw's knife too."

"He sure is. That knife has made a name for itself."

Doc extended a fold of money out of the darkness and asked Josh to take it and use it on their new ranch. He said, "Use this in getting started up. I hate to take money for another man's work." He laughed as he said it and Josh laughed along with him. "Now tell me how I can get to the new ranch. I want to take a look at it from a distance."

Josh told him the direction to take and they said their farewells. When he stood to walk back in the house, he heard the lone horse leaving from behind the barn.

Doc felt at ease as he rode into the night. His mind began to drift back to his early days. Jake Haddok had arrived in the Brazos river country of Texas with a woman and two children that were the love of his life. His wife Sarah had been a force in his life from the day he met her. He met her as a young gunman with a growing reputation. He had killed two men in gunfights. Both had left him no recourse. He had grown up in the Tennessee mountains with a gun in his hand. His rifle, and later his pistol, had become as much a part of him as his eyes and hands. His daddy, Reedus Haddok, had sent him away from home with the hope that his reputation would not follow. He had met Sarah while working for her father on a ranch in Arkansas. They fell in love and were married within a year of his leaving

Tennessee. After their marriage, they stayed on and helped her family work the ranch.

A year later Tess was born. She became the joy of their lives. Two years later Reed was born. They had their son. When they left Arkansas and headed for Texas the kids were eight and six. Their leaving was a result of Jake getting caught up in a land dispute between Sarah's father, Walt Higgins, and a large rancher, who was trying to squeeze him off his range land. A group of riders had caught Jake and Walt out on the range and threatened to burn them out if they didn't leave. Jake was wearing his pistol and he called their bluff. When the dust settled, three men were dead. Walt Higgins could not believe his eyes. Jake Haddok was something else with a gun. Word spread and he became involved in three other range wars. He settled them with his sixgun. He was always on the side of right and his reputation was one of respect.

He knew it was only a matter of time until his luck would run out. He loaded up his family and headed for Texas. After settling on their ranch, he thought his life would take a peaceful turn. A year later, he was traced down by a representative of a town in Missouri that was desperate for help in restoring law and order. The appeal was touching and the money was more than he could make on the ranch in a year's time. He took the job with the understanding that his name would never be revealed. The man "Doc" was born. Only Sarah and a few trusted friends would ever know. His wanderings that Tess and Reed would come to experience had started.

After sixteen such jobs, the name Doc had become widely known, but little was known about the man. He developed a discreet system of getting mail and messages addressed to Doc through a trusted friend in Fort Worth. He didn't mind the work because he always made sure the cause was right. It didn't bother him that the money was good.

As Doc rode on toward his son's new ranch, he recollected the time he first met Josh Spencer. It was on his sixth job, in a two-bit town, in west Texas. He had got in a showdown with four gunmen and his odds of survival were slim. Suddenly a stranger walked out into the street to stand beside him as he faced the four men. When the smoke cleared, all four were dead. The stranger's only reason for risking his life was, "You looked like you needed some help." Josh Spencer instantly became a trusted friend. He had accompanied Jake on most of his jobs since.

When Reed left for the Arizona territory, it was quite natural for Jake to call on his friend again. He had said, "Spence, trail him and make sure he lives to grow up." He would never be able to repay Josh Spencer.

At daybreak Doc sat on a hill overlooking the Rocking H. He had his glass on two riders making their way up a knoll to the right of his position. He would know his son anywhere. He had taught him how to ride. He watched him and the pretty girl dismount and stand watching the sunrise. If he had been close enough to hear, he would have heard Bud say, "I'm going to make this a fine ranch. Me and Josh will pour our lives into making it pay off."

Sam looked at him from the side and felt a twinge of pain as she saw the healing scars of his fight with Beecham. She saw the calmness in his eyes and the pride in his face. He turned to look at her and smiled that smile that made her heart melt.

She said, "Thank you for bringing me here this morning. This is a beautiful place."

"You're welcome, mam'," he grinned.

She laughed and stepped closer to him. They held each other's hand.

He asked, "Do you think your father would mind if I come calling over at the Diamond?"

"I don't think he would mind at all."

They stood close, watching the sun come up.

Doc put his glass back in his saddlebags and mounted his horse. He pulled him around to start down off the hill heading east. He looked back again, thinking, every father wants his son to grow up and be a man. My son is a man. It felt good down inside. His eyes felt a little wet. It must be the morning air. He nudged his horse with his knees and said lowly, "Come on boy. Let's head for Texas."

The day Beecham rode away from the Bar J was easily the worst day of his life. His horrible home life and the beatings his father had given him was easy compared to how he felt now. His early days as a boy existing on scraps of food and sleeping in alcoves along the waterfront of New Orleans were fond memories when contrasted with the shameful reality of what had just happened to him.

He rode bareback, in total nakedness, for about three hours. His immediate fear and relief at leaving the presence of the man called Haddok had been replaced with physical pain and emotional anger. He was a sulking and wounded warrior, seething with only one thought. Revenge!

Staying off existing trails and yet hanging close enough to them to follow their general route, he pointed himself toward New Mexico. If he could only get to Santa Fe. There he had another identity that would conceal him. There he had a large sum of money in three different bank accounts. He had contacts and influence that would allow him to chart a course of action that would leave Reed Haddok dead. His anger drove him on.

The temperature began to drop as nightfall neared. Beecham began to shake as the night air hit his body. He had to find some place to hole up. His only hope until he did was to keep moving. Just about the time it grew dark he noticed the lights of a cabin tucked away against a hill. He drew up and studied it. He could make out a barn and corral in the faint light. He had no gun so he couldn't ride in and take what he needed. He was naked so he couldn't just go down there as a traveling cowhand.

His only hope was to slip down and try to find some way to get out of the cold. The barn was his best bet. He hid his horse so he wouldn't be noticed come daylight and began to sneak toward the barn. He hoped they didn't have any dogs about that would warn the people inside.

He could hear some noise from the house, but there was no sign of anyone outside. He slipped through a door of the barn and found himself in total darkness. Standing still and adjusting his eyes, he finally saw a blanket hanging from a peg on the wall. He took it and moved toward some steps up to the loft. When on that level, he moved over into the hay near the front wall. He could look through the cracks in the boards to see the lights from the house.

He burrowed down into the hay, wrapped in the blanket. He soon felt the warmth circling his cold body. For the first time he felt like he might survive. He soon dozed off and slept fitfully through the night. He had wounds that needed tending and aches that ran completely through him. He was miserable. One of his brief periods of sleep was shattered by the slamming of a door. He opened his eyes to find sunlight streaking through the cracks of the east wall of the barn. He had survived the longest night of his life.

Peeking through the crack, he spotted a man walking toward the barn. He became motionless as the man neared the door. He was a big fellow and he was wearing a pistol. Beecham saw the man's shadow pass below him and heard what he knew to be the falling poles that served as a gate to the corral. The man was catching up his horse.

A short time later he heard the man lead the horse to the front of the barn. From the noise below him he made out the man taking a saddle through the door. He listened to the familiar sounds of a horse being saddled. The man then came back into the barn and filled a pan with some grain. Dumping it into a trough, he threw the pan back inside the door, closed it, and walked back to the house. He stopped in the yard to relieve himself before entering the house.

Beecham remained still as he listened to the horse eating. He thought to himself, could I be lucky enough for this man to ride away and leave the house unprotected? About thirty minutes later the door slammed again and he walked to the horse, swung into the saddle, and rode away.

Beecham eased down the steps from the loft and stood inside the barn door. He listened carefully as he watched the cabin. He heard nothing. With the blanket wrapped around his body, he stepped out and walked quietly to the cabin. Sneaking a look through the window, he found the one room cabin empty. He eased the door open and stepped inside.

The smell of food filled the room. He walked quickly to the stove and took some sourdough from a pan and drug it through the grease left in a skillet. He stuffed the bread in his mouth and gulped it down as he poured some still-warm coffee into a tin cup. He drank the coffee and continued to eat the bread.

Finishing, he turned to the clothes laying on the floor. He found some britches that were too large, but they were better than nothing. A shirt and some socks were dirty and bore the stench of sweat and body filth. It was sickening. He fought the urge to retch. He scrambled around looking for some boots. He found an old pair of high top lace-up shoes and put them on They were better than being barefoot. He found no coat. He cut a head hole in a blanket to use as a coat.

Scrambling through the food he found three cans of beans. He threw them into a sack along with a small knife he found on the table. His final search produced sixty-five cents in coins. He left the house with his loot over his shoulder and walked back to the barn. A quick search revealed no saddle. The blanket he used to keep warm during the night would have to do. He made his way to his horse and left immediately. He was a sight to look at, but a lot better off than yesterday.

His next stop was three days later at a small settlement in New

Mexico. It was a place where the stagecoach stopped. He managed to sell the horse and buy a ticket east on the stage. He had enough money left to buy some clothes and boots. A bath and some salve for the cuts on his face left him with just enough money for a meal and some food on the stage route. He was on his way to Santa Fe.

Beecham arrived four days later. They had traveled day and night, only stopping for brief meals and a change of horses. His face still looked a mess with large scabs and a swollen nose. He avoided the stares and questions of the other passengers and stayed within himself the entire trip. His mind was busy with hatred for Haddok. He was plotting. By the time the stage pulled into Santa Fe, he knew what he would do.

When he got off the stage, he walked quickly away from the crowd and hailed a carriage. He gave the driver an address on the west side of town and sat back to observe the life of the town. He had left here about two years ago with plans of greatness. Those plans were now in shambles.

When the carriage stopped in front of a large stone house that was set back from the road, he paid the driver and walked to the door. It was locked. He knocked and the door was opened by a Mexican woman.

"Hello, Rosetta," Beecham said.

"Mr. Lain," she said excitedly. You look awful. What has happened to you?"

"I've had some problems. I'll be staying here for a while. Is Pablo here?"

"He's out back working on the hedge row. Should I get him?"

"I'm going to get a bath and a change of clothes. Tell him I want to see him in about one hour."

"Yes sir! It's good to have you home."

Beecham went to his bedroom and began to undress. He could hear Rosetta preparing his bath in the next room. Later, as he settled into the water and began to soak, he thought of the man Frank Lain he was known as in Santa Fe. It was a respected name and he had influential friends in many of the right places. Most knew that he had been away on extended business. It would be easy for him to move back into their circles. However, he would have to wait until his wounds healed. He did not want to answer questions.

His thoughts shifted to Haddok. He wanted to initiate his plan as soon as possible. He dressed quickly and went to his study where he found Pablo waiting.

Pablo stood as he entered and addressed his boss politely, "Good morning, Mr. Lain."

"Good morning, Pablo. I've got some urgent business for you to tend to."

He found a sheet of paper and scribbled a note that he folded and placed in an envelope. He sealed it and wrote the name of Will Malone on the outside. The note said,

Contact Ike Craven and have him meet
me at my house as soon as possible.
Keep this quiet.

He signed it, F. Lain. Handing the envelope to Pablo, he said, "Go to the Empire saloon and ask for Will Malone. He is a gambler that hangs out there. Give him, and him alone, this message. Tell him to let me know of his progress."

117

Pablo took the note and left immediately. At the saloon he found Mr. Malone. Malone opened the envelope and read its contents. Pablo told him of Mr. Lain's desire to know of his progress. Malone thought for a moment and then responded.

"Tell Mr. Lain that it will probably take a couple of days, but no more."

Pablo thanked him and left. He returned and gave his boss the message. It seemed to please Mr. Lain.

Two days later, in the middle of the afternoon, Rosetta knocked at Lain's study and told him a mister Ike Craven was there to see him. He told her to show him in.

Ike Craven walked into the room and Rosetta closed the door. Craven's appearance gave him away. He was in his late twenties and had the bearing of a man who was sure of himself. He wore two pistols tied down. He was good with both. In the Missouri country he was the best. He loved his reputation and enjoyed the fact that men were scared of him. He was for hire and Beecham had used his services before. In Beecham's mind there was none better than Ike Craven.

"Hello Ike," Beecham said.

"Man! You look like you've been run over by a bull. What happened to you?"

"That's no concern of yours Ike. I've got a job for you. There's a man by the name of Haddok who lives near Prescott in the Arizona territory. I want him dead."

"That's not a problem. How bad do you want him dead?"`

"One thousand now and another thousand when the job is done."

118

"You've got yourself a deal. Is there anything you need to tell me about Haddok?"

"You'll find him on the Bar J ranch. He's good, but he's no match for you. I want it done as soon as possible."

Beecham wrote him out a note and told him to take it to the bank and give it to the manager. He told Craven that the note would get him his first thousand.

Craven took the note and left. On the way out, he turned and said to Beecham, "Get the rest of your money ready. I'll be back to collect."

Beecham saw him out and returned to sit in his favorite chair. A smile broke across his healing face as he saw the picture in his mind of Haddok laying in the dirt, drawing his last breath. He wished he could be there to witness it.

As Ike Craven walked to the bank, he thought, Haddok must be special to Lain. He had never made two thousand dollars for killing a man.

Doc was eight days out of Prescott when he rode into the small settlement of Cedar Creek. It was a gathering of a few families that had developed a productive business along one of the main routes west. The houses and establishments flanked a small intermittent creek that only looked like a creek when there was a lot of rainfall upstream. There was a general store and a cafe that doubled as a saloon. A blacksmith shop was the primary attraction for travelers. A headcount of the regulars in the settlement would not reach fifty. There was no law. A man could rent a bunk, get a bath, and a good meal for a fair price. Doc had stopped here on his way to Prescott. He had looked forward to getting back here for the past two days.

He rode directly to the livery and left his horse for a good bait of grain. He took his gear to the bath house that also had a couple of rooms with bunks. He paid for both and enjoyed a long bath. After he dressed, he walked to the cafe to get something to eat.

It was getting late in the day as he walked in and took a table in the corner. The supper crowd was gathering and the place was buzzing with talk. Eight men stood at the bar on the other side of the room. They were talking quietly and enjoying their drinks. All of them appeared to be local folk. None were wearing pistols.

Most of the tables were taken by men and women who were eating. A young woman was waiting on the tables and they were all calling her Jenny. She knew them all it seemed and was enjoying her work. An older man was working behind the bar and an older woman was busy in the kitchen. Doc figured them to be family. It made him proud to see a family working hard and making it in life.

Jenny came to his table and told him all they had to offer. He settled for some fried steak and beans. As he sipped his coffee and waited on the food, he began to relax and enjoy the sound of people around him. His food came in a few minutes and he dug in.

It was good. While he was eating, he caught the movement of someone entering the door. He looked that way and saw a neatly dressed young man who looked to be in his twenties. He wore matching colts tied down. He scanned the room and Doc dropped his head just before the man got to his part of the room. Doc glanced again as he looked away and sized him up as a gunslinger. By that time the entire cafe had noticed his presence and grew quiet. You could tell he liked the attention. He broke the silence.

"I'm Ike Craven. I want to get a drink and something to eat. Stay out of my way and you'll be all right."

The crowd began to buzz again and a few people paid up and left. Craven walked cockily over to a table near Doc and loudly told the bartender to bring him a bottle of whiskey. Doc kept his head down and continued to eat. Doc thought, so this is Ike Craven. He knew the name and the reputation. The talk was that he might be the fastest gun alive. What was he doing here?

Doc continued to eat and mind his own business. Jenny brought Craven a bottle and left the table. He poured a drink and sat looking the room over. His eyes and attention were obviously centered on Jenny. He followed her every move. When she came back to take his order, he grabbed her hand and made her stand at his table.

"I may just take you to Prescott with me and show you a good time."

"Please let me go Mr. Craven. I've got a lot of work to do." Jenny was trying to get away from him without causing a problem.

"Your job right now is to make me happy," Craven replied. "Believe me, you don't want me unhappy." He released his grip on her hand and she quickly left.

The man behind the bar, who Doc figured to be Jenny's father, had been watching the encounter. He didn't like it but he stayed behind the bar.

Doc tried to keep his eyes off Craven and his ears open. He was wondering why Craven was going to Prescott. The fact that his son was there and Craven was a known gun for hire made him more interested.

When Jenny brought the food, Craven demanded that she sit at his table while he ate.

Jenny protested, "I can't. I've got to wait on these other people."

"You set down, or I'll clear everybody but you and me out of here."

She reluctantly sat down. She was nervously looking back toward the bar. It was obvious that she didn't want trouble.

Craven began to talk. "I've got a little job to do in Prescott. When I'm through, I'm going to come back by here. If you are nice to me, I'll bring you a present."

"I don't want any presents. Besides, I don't know you."

"Oh! You'll get to know me. I've got lots of women who want to spend time with me. You'll love it."

Trying to change the subject, Jenny asked him, "What kind of work do you do?"

"I kill people," he said with a smile. "You mean you have never heard of me?"

Jenny responded, "No, I haven't."

"Well, you will. I get rid of people that somebody is willing to pay good money to see dead. I'm setting here talking to you with nearly a thousand dollars in my pocket because somebody wants a man dead."

"Oh, my goodness. I don't think I need to be hearing this. I can't believe you could be so cold about a person's life."

"It's all about money. There's a man named Haddok in Prescott that don't have long to live. I don't know him. I have no feelings for him. He represents money to me." Craven was doing his best to impress Jenny.

Doc listened and his fear was correct. This gunslinger had been hired to kill his son. There was no way he was going to let Ike Craven leave Cedar Creek. Without any indication, his interest left his food and his senses became alive. He adjusted his pistol beneath the table. A casual look would have revealed Doc as completely disinterested. However, his mind was running. How will it happen? How would he choose his time?

His thoughts were interrupted by the sound of the man who worked behind the bar as he walked over to Craven's table.

"Jenny, get up and get to work," the man said. "We've got people who are waiting on their food." Jenny looked frightened.

Craven stood up and held his hands out over his pistols. He spoke loudly, so everyone in the room could hear. "You and all the rest of these people get out of here. I've decided I want to eat with this woman and I don't want to be bothered." He hesitated a few seconds and then continued. "If you don't all leave now, I'm going to start shooting."

The man walked away and the people started hurriedly leaving the cafe. Craven watched for a minute, feeling mighty big. He was sitting back down when he noticed the lone man at the table to his side.

"Hey, you! Get out of here. What's the matter with you? Can't you hear?"

Doc stood and stepped beside his table, facing Craven. Calmly, and with complete disregard, he spoke, "I can hear. I hear a mighty little man trying to sound big. I'm not leaving til I get ready, and you are not leaving at all."

For the first time Craven noticed the man had his gun tied down. He tried to place the man's face, but he had never seen him before. The man's eyes were like steel and it was obvious he wasn't afraid. Surely the man, if he was a gunfighter, had heard of Ike Craven. If he had, then why wasn't he afraid? Craven didn't show it so it would be noticed, but it made him a little uncertain. It was a feeling he hadn't felt in a long time.

Craven pushed his chair back and stood up. Jenny walked quickly toward the bar. Footsteps could be heard outside as people gathered at the door and window to watch. Ike Craven and Doc stood facing each other with only about eight feet between them.

Craven broke the silence. "I'm giving you one more chance to walk out."

Doc answered, "Why should I leave when there's no other place in the world I'd rather be."

Craven nervously licked his lips and thought of the reality of his situation. At this close range it was likely they both would be killed. He hadn't really planned on anything like this. He shuffled his feet a little and lowered his hands until they were hovering over the bone handles of his pistols. The other man was just standing there, relaxed and seemingly unconcerned. Craven started his usual banter that always preceded his draw. He had used it so many times to unnerve his opponent and gain an edge.

"I don't know who you are," Craven said, "but I'll see you get a good burial. I'm going to count to—"

In the middle of Craven's talking, in a move that resembled a flash of lightning, Doc drew and fired two rapid shots into Craven's chest. Craven had dropped his hands to draw, but he was late. The power of the slugs threw him backward and he landed on his back. Blood was bubbling out of his chest as he felt the weakness of death creeping over his body. His eyes were going dim when he looked up at the man standing over him. He struggled to talk and finally muttered these words.

"Who are you?"

Doc looked down at him and spoke in a voice so low that no one else could hear, "Just a man that kept you from getting killed in Prescott. The name's Haddok."

Cravens eyes widened in surprise. He then coughed and died. Doc reached into Craven's pockets and found the money he had been paid to kill his son. He threw a hundred dollars on the table and said to the owner of the cafe as they spilled back inside, "Use that to bury him. You can sell his horse and gear and keep the money."

Doc walked through the people and out the door. He went immediately to pick up his gear and then to the livery. He saddled his horse, mounted up, and was heading out of town when the cafe owner and a group of men stopped him.

The cafe owner spoke. "Ike Craven was known everywhere. People will want to know who killed him. Who are you?"

"Just tell them it was a man who didn't cut Ike Craven no slack."

With that, Doc nudged his horse through the men and down the street. As he headed out of town he thought to himself, I wish I was in Texas.